BY DAWN

PERSEPHONE AUTUMN WRITING AS
P. AUTUMN

BY DAWN

P. AUTUMN

BETWEEN WORDS PUBLISHING LLC

By Dawn

ISBN: 978-1-951477-10-3 (Ebook)

ISBN: 978-1-951477-11-0 (Paperback)

Editor: Ellie McLove | My Brother's Editor

Proofreader: Rosa Sharon | My Brother's Editor

Cover Design: Abigail Davies | Pink Elephant Designs

Here's to the group chat…
Nellie, Kristine, Scott, Jill, Brenda, and Jessica.
And to Nanci for her love of dogs.

Thank you all for blowing up my wife's phone, annoying the hell
out of me, and inspiring this book.

Cheers and enjoy!

BOOKS BY PERSEPHONE AUTUMN

Standalone Romance Novels

Depths Awakened

Sweet Tooth (January 2021)

Devotion Series

Distorted Devotion

Undying Devotion

Beloved Devotion

Bay Area Duet Series

Click Duet

Through The Lens (April 2021)

Time Exposure (June 2021)

Inked Duet

Fine Line (September 2021)

Love Buzz (November 2021)

Poetry Collections

Ink Veins

Standalone Horror Novels

By Dawn (P. Autumn)

PREFACE

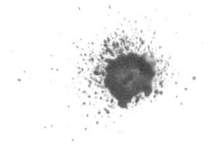

This book in written in narrative third person as well as multiple, individual, first person points of view. If, at the start of a chapter, there is no character name, it is narrative POV. If a character is listed at the beginning of a chapter or after a break, it will be in that POV.

PROLOGUE

CAPTOR

IT WAS ALL JUST A GAME. A vicious game I loved to play. A devilish game I would never live without. Couldn't live without. And at the end of the day, I always rang victoriously.

What was the game, you ask?

Lean in close. Closer.

One never comprehended the game until it was too late. One never processed the game until their life flashed before their eyes.

It was all just a game. A glorious game.

But oh, how I loved to play.

CHAPTER ONE

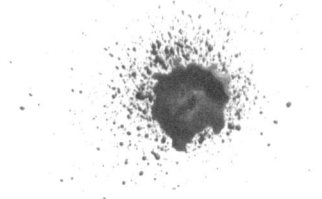

A GROAN ECHOED off the walls in the dimly lit dank space, the reverberation heavy with sleep. A petite, blonde woman rolled onto her back, the couch protesting beneath her weight as coils dug into the thin skin at her spine. Reaching for her forehead with a delicate hand, she pinched the bridge of her nose as her eyes clamped tighter.

Cymbals clanged in her head as she tried to remember what happened last. What she had done to create this torturous state. Her mouth drier than the time she suffered heatstroke at the beach. Nose scrunched from a nearby odor —an unfamiliar and unappealing funk. Like must or mildew or rotting wood.

None of it made sense.

A moan bellowed, stole the moment and silenced the clanging in her head. The gruff tone erupted from the back side of the weathered couch.

The blonde's eyes flashed open; pupils fully dilated. She held her breath, not daring enough to exhale. Shadows danced on the walls as light filtered in from various corners of the space. Not artificial light. Moonlight. But from where exactly?

Another moan. Magnetized to the couch, her eyes locked on the ceiling as she prayed.

Zeroing in on the ceiling, a new awareness washed over the woman as she squinted at the dusty fleur-de-lis pattern above her. Casting her line of sight lower, she scanned the moldy wallpaper as it peeled away from the wall in various places.

Where the hell am I? she thought.

The blonde remained rooted on the couch and waited. She wondered if the person responsible for the foreign moan would make themselves known. Jump up with a *gotcha*.

Glued to the couch, refusing to move an inch, her eyes trailed to the backrest and noticed the material was all wrong. Pea-green fabric stared back at her. Dingy and tattered. A few spots torn away as her vision traced closer toward her feet. Scratchy beneath the bare areas of her flesh. A thin film layer coated the couch surface and smeared against her skin.

She squinted briefly as nausea rolled up her throat.

The moan echoed in the room once more. Her eyes shifted from the dank, green couch to the chipping paint on the ceiling tiles. Nothing about this place was familiar. Not a single thing. Pain seared her palms and spread up her arms as she balled her fingers into fists and dug her nails in the flesh. Fear slowly seeped into her veins as unease settled in her gut.

Unsure of where she was, only one fact held true. She was not alone.

Gingerly, she eased herself upright. Each inch she shifted was a new game of not allowing the couch springs to creak under her weight. The moaner didn't need to know she existed. Not quite yet. Feet planted on the floor, she stretched her neck left and right. Another scan of the musky room sent a shiver up her spine.

Cobwebs layered the walls like a fresh coat of paint. Dust and a grimy sheen blanketed the furniture surfaces. From somewhere behind her, moonlight trickled in and highlighted the occasional piece of furniture—which was severely outdated. But the smell. The funk emanating from every inch of the room made her hold her breath at every opportunity.

Standing up, she took a step to the left. Then another. And another. The wood floor protested with each of her steps. Easing her pace, she methodically stepped past the couch arm and halted in her tracks.

Difficult to see in the dim light, the blonde rubbed her eyes. She didn't know if her mind played tricks on her. But she swore another woman laid beside the couch on the floor. An unfamiliar woman with a petite frame and pixie-cut hazelnut hair. Maybe weighed a hundred pounds soaking wet.

Another moan vibrated from the small woman on the floor. One of her hands lifting to clutch the front of her head at the hairline, a noticeable gash on her right cheek. The blonde stepped back a few feet to add more distance between them. Alternating her weight left and right, the blonde cleared her throat in an effort to signal her presence to the woman still stretched across the floor.

The petite woman shielded her eyes with a hand. Her eyes scanned the room, searching for the source of the sound. Spotting the blonde, the petite woman dug her heels into the floor and scooted farther away.

"Who are you?" the blonde asked, her voice scraping the air like sandpaper.

The blonde's eyes pinched slightly as she searched the face of the other woman. An uncomfortable silence thick in the air as neither uttered a word. Each studied the other. Unanswered questions loomed over them like a gray storm cloud ready to let loose. Both of them seeking and failing to understand what led them here.

Unsatisfied with the lack of conversation, the blonde spoke up. "Name's Billie. You?" Billie waved in greeting. "Happen to know where the hell we are?"

The brunette glimpsed Billie head to toe. Billie appeared every bit as uncomfortable as the brunette felt. Arms hugged tight around her midsection. Fingers clenched into tight fists and clutching the cotton of her knee-length, white dress. Legs shifting weight every other breath. Eyes jumpy. Jaw rigid with tension. Her greeting ignored.

Lowering her hand from her face, the brunette rose to sit upright.

"I'm..." The brunette paused as her voice cracked.

She reached for her throat, wrapping both hands around her esophagus as she swallowed heavily. Swishing her tongue in her mouth, she built up an inkling of saliva and swallowed again. This time when she spoke, her voice was less hoarse.

"I'm Kelly. Are we still at Carrie's house?" Kelly took in her surroundings for the first time. The house not as she last remembered.

"Who the hell is Carrie?" Billie asked as she hugged herself tighter.

Kelly steadily rose from the floor. Once on her feet, she stretched her limbs and twisted her back left and right. A popping rippled from her spine, followed by her neck. Kelly's eyes skirted the room. With every piece of furniture and speck of dust she identified, a new layer of confusion settled in her bones.

"Carrie. I was at her party last night. Or tonight. What day is it?" Kelly rubbed a palm against her forehead. "This is *definitely* not her place."

Kelly rounded the couch as her eyes continually searched the room for any clues as to their location. In front of the couch was an oval wooden table with wobbly legs. Lying dead center on the table was an envelope. Flashing like a light on a slot machine. Begging for attention. Kelly instinctively picked up the envelope, bringing the thin rectangle closer in the dimly lit room.

Open Me When All Seven Are Awake

Kelly's brow shot closer to her hairline and cinched the skin. Small ridges and valleys landscaped her forehead.

Billie stood off to the side and soaked up Kelly's confusion for a beat. When Kelly gave no explanation for the envelope, Billie sidled up next to her and read the front of the tattered, manila envelope.

"*When all seven are awake?*" Billie glanced up to Kelly's face. Eyes laser-focused on the envelope as if it might disappear if she looked away. "I don't understand. What the hell is going on?" Billie asked, her pitch edged with hysteria.

Before Kelly could respond, a loud cough bellowed from a different room of the house. Both women snapped their heads in the general direction of the sound just as a second, more gravelly cough erupted.

With the envelope still clutched in her hands, Kelly headed in the direction of where she heard the cough stem from. She waltzed through a rundown dining room. The space piqued her interest but would have to wait. The mystery cougher instantly became top priority.

Reaching the entrance of a hallway, Kelly halted in her tracks. *Oomph!* Toe to heel behind her, Billie slammed into Kelly without warning. Kelly spun around—eyes wide, brows raised, a curse on the tip of her tongue—and slapped a finger to her lips, signaling Billie to keep quiet. Billie nodded and mouthed *sorry*. Going forward, Billie swore she'd only take a step when she knew Kelly had. Stepping in line behind Kelly—as if a child shadowing a parent—Billie followed in her wake.

Illuminated only by the dim light behind them, Kelly flipped a light switch on the wall. Nothing. The hall still shrouded in darkness, she flicked the switch again and again. On the third flip, the bulb sparked to life. Billie and Kelly stammered in place as their eyes adjusted to the brightness. Slowly, both the women peeled their eyes open. As their eyes surveyed the hall and nearby dining room, a loud pop ripped through the air before darkness blanketed them once again.

Kelly dug deep to remember everything she observed while the hall was lit.

The hall stretched roughly twenty feet—three doors on the right, three doors on the left, a single door at the end. Two doors on the right rested ajar as did one on the left. 1960s blue and green, Bradbury wallpaper peeled at the seams down the corridor. A blanket of dust as thick as snow laid on the floor.

Slower than a tortoise, Kelly strode down the narrow corridor with Billie a foot behind her. Hesitant, they approached the first open door on the left. Kelly peeked over her shoulder at Billie and pressed a finger to her lips again. Billie nodded.

Peering through the cracked opening, Kelly spotted small, square tiles on the wall. Reaching forward, she bumped the door open farther. The hinges complained as the door swung open, causing Kelly and Billie to inch back.

When her eyes adjusted to the view, Kelly crept forward and touched the edge of a pedestal sink before yanking her hand away. Beside the sink was a toilet and a wide clawfoot bathtub. Stepping farther into the bathroom, she squinted to locate the fixtures in hopes of finding a working light. As her hand brushed the walls near the door, Kelly soon learned where the light switch should be was replaced with a flat, blank switch plate. And every surface her fingers grazed was coated with a grimy brown film. Every speck of porcelain layered in filth.

Backing out of the room, a shiver rippled through Kelly's body as Billie grabbed hold of her shirt hem. Leaning in, Billie whispered in Kelly's ear. "Sorry. Didn't mean to startle you."

"It's fine. This place just gives me the creeps." Kelly gestured to the next open door. "Let's see if anyone's in there."

Billie nodded and matched Kelly's stride as she headed for the next door.

As the room came into view, Kelly's gait slowed to a standing crawl. She crept to the edge of the doorway and peered around the frame. From her vantage point, she surveyed as much of the room as possible. This room was better lit than the living room they woke in. The faint illumination brightened the bedroom just enough to spy faint details. Floral wallpaper covered the drywall—heavyset with pinks, yellows, and greens—slowly peeling up at the seam lines like the living room. The pattern dizzying and enough to make a person vomit.

A dark, wooden dresser with eight large drawers butted against one of the walls—the edge of each drawer hand-carved with intricate curves and swirls. Large, gaudy handles mounted front and center of each drawer. A few feet above the chest of drawers, shelf after shelf furnished the wall and framed a large mirror. So far, every house fitting was reminiscent of a different era. A time when appliances and furnishings were made to a different standard. Sturdier. Heavier. More intricate.

Billie gasped as she scanned the shelves over Kelly's shoulder.

"What?" Kelly whisper-asked. Billie raised her arm and pointed at the shelves. Kelly squinted to decipher what Billie saw.

Each and every shelf held a plethora of porcelain dolls. No two dolls alike in appearance. Some rather dated. Others more modern. Female. Male. Young. Elderly. Middle-aged. Upon first glance, someone might guess there were nearly a hundred dolls perched on the ledges. But the number easily superseded.

The dolls were equally cute and creepy. Kelly shifted her attention away from the porcelain figures momentarily. Looking down at the mirror—the edges discolored and bubbled with a few chips and splinters in the glass—she scoped out more of the room from her vantage point.

In the mirror's reflection, she caught sight of two sets of shoes dangling from the side of a blanketed bed. She spun around to face Billie and spoke barely above a whisper. "There are people in the room. At least two I can see." She glanced back at the mirror briefly and noticed one pair of feet twitched. "I'm going in there. You can stay with me or stay in the hall. Up to you."

Without waiting for a response from Billie, Kelly stepped forward and stood in the door's archway. A man and a woman laid sideways across the king-sized mattress, neither of them familiar. She approached the bed, eager to wake the couple, but stopped short at the edge of the bed. Lying on the floor, under the feet of the two people on the bed, was another unfamiliar woman.

Glancing over her shoulder, she discovered Billie rooted at the room's entrance with her arms wrapped tightly around her chest. Kelly pointed to the floor beside the bed and mouthed *someone else is on the floor*. A hand flew up to Billie's mouth, her eyes glassed over as red lines wove webs in the whites. Her breath came in short bursts. Artery expanding and contracting erratically beside her throat. Skin gray and damp.

Kelly inched closer to the bed, reaching forward to touch the woman's arm. She nudged her gently as to not startle her. The woman rolled closer to the foot of the bed; a soft grunt emitted from her throat. Prodding her arm with a bit more force, Kelly stepped back when the woman stirred with a groan of displeasure.

The woman's eyes opened slowly. As the room came more into focus, her forehead bunched. One of her hands pressed down on the mattress as she cautiously hoisted herself upright. Short, peachy wavelets framed her face. Now sitting, the woman lifted her hands to either side of her head and massaged her temples.

As if realization suddenly struck, the woman's head tipped up. Eyes wide. Face ashen. Sweat faint above her brows. Hesitantly, the woman's eyes abandoned Kelly and bounced around the room mimicking a ping pong championship match. The more she scanned, the wider her pupils dilated. At the sight of Kelly, the woman scooted closer to the headboard, but not before she bumped into the man behind her.

Peeking behind her, the woman screamed and bolted off the bed. In the closest corner, she drew her knees to her chest and hugged them fiercely. Her screams subsided as her dry throat took precedence. But it wasn't long before her screams were followed up with sharp questions and loud accusations.

"Who *the fuck* are you? Where the hell am I? What the fuck did you do to me?"

Kelly's hands flew up beside her face. Palms forward in surrender. Voice gentle as she spoke.

"My name's Kelly. This is" —she gestured over to the doorway— "Billie. Don't have a clue where we are. Just woke you up. You okay?"

The woman straightened her legs and scanned her body, checking if anything appeared out of place. After a thorough once-over, she nodded. "Sorry for yelling. What the hell is happening? Why are we here?"

As Kelly's mouth formulated an answer, the man on the bed woke up. His cough crackling in the silence. In unison, the three women snapped their heads in his direction and watched as he sat up. Legs partially on the bed, feet dangling. Without a word, they waited for his reaction.

His right hand reached up and clutched the base of his skull as he rubbed his short, salt-and-pepper hair. A hiss escaped his lips when his hand grazed along a spot halfway up his head. He scooted closer to the edge of the bed and, before Kelly stopped him, planted his feet on what he assumed was the floor. Instantly, an ear-piercing screech echoed off the walls.

The man stumbled sideways before peering down to the floor and noticing a woman at his feet. A small woman with pecan-colored hair—the length reaching her mid-back, bangs stopping just shy of her brows—emerged from the bedside floor space. She gripped the bed frame and heaved herself upright. Enveloping herself in her own arms, she rubbed a hand over her now bruised bicep.

Before any of them uttered another word, a voice intercepted from somewhere outside of the bedroom.

"Hello? Is anyone there?" a female voice called out.

Footsteps clacked louder and louder in the hall as the group of five stood in the bedroom. Five pairs of eyes aimed toward the hallway. Waiting.

Another call floated in the air. "Hello?"

The five stood motionless. Absolutely silent. Not so patiently waiting to learn who the voice belonged to. Heavy shoes clapped on the hardwood floor. Growing closer. Louder. The small group clambered closer together to work as a unit against the unknown.

A dark-haired woman popped her head in the room. A soft smile stretched wide on her face as she spied the group in the room. On her heel was an olive-skinned brunette.

Kelly scanned the room and counted everyone in her head. *Seven.* She stepped forward and inched closer to the center of the room where everyone had a clear shot of her. Holding the envelope up for everyone to see, she spoke to the six people gathered in the room.

"We should head back to the living room. Someone left a note."

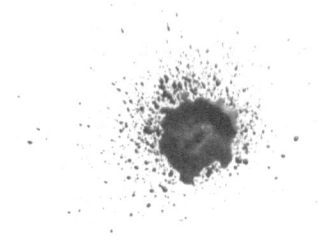

The seven strangers gathered in the dim light of the dank living room. As she headed for the couch, Billie noticed a light switch on the far wall. *It never hurts to try,* she thought. Steering in its direction, she reached out and flipped the switch up when she neared. Nothing. No flickers. No light. Not a single bulb came on. So, she flipped it off and on. Once. Twice. Three times. Again, nothing.

Billie didn't want to give up, but she also had no desire to flip a light switch up and down for no reason. So, for now, she threw in the towel.

Before finagling a spot to sit among the six strangers, Billie ambled to a pair of drawn curtains. Tugging the tattered, dusty material back, she coughed as the outside light filtered in through dark yellow-tinged window panes. The light glow minimal, but it wiped away the darkness enough to be seen.

Billie sat on the couch next to Kelly and gazed at the five other individuals she hadn't formally met. Not that Billie and Kelly had an ideal introduction. She studied each of their faces briefly as she searched her mind's eye for a way to connect them. Not a single iota of recognition clicked as she studied each of them. Not one of them noticeably similar in appearance.

How odd, she thought.

Kelly held the envelope up for everyone to see. "Earlier, when Billie and I woke up in this room, we stumbled across this envelope. It says to open it when all seven of us are awake."

The woman with the dark hair raised her hand as if in grade school. Kelly paused and acknowledged her with a chin lift.

"Hi. I'm Jennifer." A warm smile curved the corners of her mouth and outer edges of her eyes. She waved like the Queen of England to everyone in the semi-circle—almost three-quarters circle—around the coffee table. "What do you mean, the envelope says to open it when all seven of us are awake?"

Kelly held up the envelope, flashing the words away from her and swiveling it side-to-side so everyone can see the writing on the exterior. "Exactly what I said," she stated sarcastically.

The man snatched the envelope from Kelly's grip, eager to tear the worn corners and reveal the contents inside. "Gimme that. Let's see what this bullshit says."

His stubby fingers tore at the flap, shredding the top of the yellowed exterior. Spreading the pocket of the envelope wide, he removed the folded papers hidden inside. Gingerly, he unfolded the pages and brought the note closer as his eyes scanned the handwritten scrawl in fountain ink.

"What does it say?" the small woman whom the man stepped on earlier asked.

He peeked over the top of the pages for a brief moment before returning his focus to the words in front of him. Clearing his throat, he read the note aloud.

Dear Lucky Seven,

I brought each of you here for a different reason. No two reasons are the same. So, do yourself a favor and don't try to compare each other to find commonalities. I promise you will not be successful. I have been watching each of you for some time now. Pet projects, if you will. Each of you has something that attracted me from day one. So, I've brought you here, to this house, so I can keep a better eye on all of you. While you're here, I suggest you make yourselves at home. Be yourself. Be comfortable. Live how you normally would do so. I stockpiled the kitchen pantry and there are enough amenities for you to survive here for some time. When I feel my desires for each of you has been satiated, I plan to set you free. Until that day arrives, though, you belong to me. Don't try to leave. You will find the fruits of your labor unsuccessful. Only I hold the power to let you leave. Remember... just be yourselves. That's all I want. Soon, your time here will end.

D

"What in the ever-loving fuck is that supposed to mean?" The man's voice boomed and broke the awestruck expression on each person's face. As he continued, his voice grew louder the more he spoke. "Just be ourselves and this

P. AUTUMN

sick fuck will let us go. This is fucking bullshit! A goddamn joke!"

The olive-skinned woman next to him ripped the letter from his hand and read it herself, tossing each of the pages onto the table as she finished. "Obviously we're trapped in some sick, psychopath's version of playtime. Maybe, between the seven of us, we can outsmart this whacked-out son of a bitch."

A few heads in the group bobbed up and down, agreeing with the woman. The woman with the pecan-colored hair spoke up next. "Like to think that's possible. I'm sure we're all good at something and we can help each other in figuring a way out of this."

"Okay. In order to figure out a plan, while acting *normal* for this clown, we need to know more about each other," Kelly suggested. "So, let's meet each other. My name's Kelly. I'm a tattoo artist. Last thing I remember was being at a friend's party and laying down because I was too drunk to do anything else. Next thing I know, I'm on the floor behind this couch being woken up by Billie." She pointed to the blonde beside her. "I only know her name because she told me."

The only blonde in the room raised her hand and took it upon herself to share next.

"Hey everybody, I'm Billie. Work as a waitress at a mom-and-pop diner on Highway 95. Last thing I remember was walking off the makeshift stage in a bar near my house. I had just finished singing my sixth karaoke song and went to the bar for a drink." She taps her throat. "Parched from all the singing. The bartender slid an appletini in front of

18

me, my favorite drink, and I hadn't ordered yet. When I asked him how he knew my drink of choice, he told me a man who watched my performance paid for my drink before leaving. Honestly... I remember very little after drinking it."

For a moment, Billie sat pensively. Her thoughts cycled through a million various images of men she'd seen in the bar last night. She had barely given it much thought after her first sip of the cocktail. Now, she scanned through every still image in her mind like an old movie projector as she tried recalling anyone overly interested in her.

Nothing but blank images popped up.

Assuming she would be the next to speak, the espresso-brown haired woman—who had introduced herself as Jennifer not long ago—shared her story. "As I said before, I'm Jennifer. I'm a lab technician for Veather Works." A sea of confused strangers stared at Jennifer. This occurred anytime Jennifer told someone where she worked. "Basically, the company manufactures leatherlike products from non-animal sources. Vegan leather. Veather. Anyway... I was working until four in the morning and decided I needed to sleep a little before I drove home. So, I fell asleep in my car with a plan to wake up after an hour of rest. Next thing I know, I'm waking up in some smelly, dank-ass bed next to her."

Jennifer pointed to the woman on her left. The olive-toned woman shrugged, and her thick, black, wavy hair naturally swept away from her face, uncovering previously undetectable bruises.

Following the lead of those before her and continuing

the circle of introductions, the olive-skinned woman spoke next. "My name is Belinda. Work at the Fill N' Munch about a mile from Highway 64. I'm the evening shift manager. Normally, I work until eleven, but last night I stayed later. The manager set to relieve me; his daughter had a high fever. Ended up leaving around a quarter to three in the morning. I remember being on the highway, a few exits away from mine, when a car appeared out of nowhere. It rode my bumper, nudging me a couple times. Really scared me as I tried to get away. The last thing I recall is my car leaving the roadway and my foot mashing the brakes in an attempt to not hit a utility post." Pointing to the bruises covering her face and neck, she continued. "Must have hit something. Otherwise, how would I have all these bruises? None of you have bruises... do you?"

Unmoving, they simply stared at each other for a moment. Then, as if someone flipped a switch in their heads, they snapped out of their daydreams. One by one, each person in the circle scanned the length of their arms. Inspected every inch for something out of place. Abnormal. Next, they did the same with their legs. Finished examining their limbs, anyone with other exposed skin checked the remainder. Not a single one of them had visible marks.

Belinda sagged into the dingy couch and hung her head. She wallowed over how no one else was physically harmed. But she wasn't alone. The man rubbed the base of his skull, running his fingers lightly over the short salt-and-pepper strands on the back of his scalp. Eyes narrowed, he bared his teeth and hissed when he grazed a tender spot.

Six sets of eyes landed on him like flies on shit.

"What?" he asked, brow tugged together. All eyes on him, unblinking. Not a word spoken. He fidgeted in his seat before continuing. "There's a lump on the back of my head. Not a bruise. Totally different." A few of the women nodded, and the man took the small acceptance as a sign to introduce himself.

"*Hell-ooo*, ladies. Name's Skip. And I think I'm the luckiest fucking guy on the planet right now. Yeah, it sucks we're all stuck in this house, but at least I've got some fine-ass eye candy while we wait for this shit to end."

Five of the six women shared similar reactions—eyes peered to the heavens, heads methodically shook as displeasure rolled off them in waves. The simple fact that some maniac forced them to stay in this ghastly place with a chauvinist was beyond irritation.

One woman, though, sat transfixed by Skip. She hung on to every word he spoke and silently begged for more.

"Or... maybe not." Skip winked at Billie and smiled devilishly as her cheeks pinked. "As I was saying. I'm a locksmith and am quite certain we'll be able to get out of this shithole with me here. Last thing I remember..." He tapped his chin and closed his eyes, as if remembering prior events was challenging. "Ah, yes. I was on a date with the fine-as-hell Deanna. Unfortunately, the date ended sooner than desirable. Pissed her off that my age on the hookup site was off by a few years."

Disinterested or not, every woman in the circle leaned forward. Expectant expressions on their faces as they silently waited for Skip to elaborate. "So what if my profile says I'm thirty-three. Not like it's that far from forty-seven.

And I think my body's better than most younger men." Skip patted his stomach for effect. "Anyway, twenty-year-old Deanna became upset and stormed off. I stayed at the restaurant and ate in the hopes of making up for my date bailing. I remember unlocking my car, but nothing after."

"Maybe she smacked your lying ass in the back of the head when you weren't looking. I know I would have," Kelly professed. Skip snarled while Kelly pursed her lips and raised her brows in challenge.

And then laughter broke out. Light at first, but growing with each passing second. The loudest emanating from Kelly. Skip followed her crack with a poor attempt at rebuttal. "Can't help I'm a satyromaniac. I like sex and I'll take the measures necessary to get it. Age is just a number, baby."

Kelly rolled her eyes at his lewdness. "Whatever, man." She glanced at the peachy-haired woman sitting to Skip's left, gesturing a hand in her direction and suggesting she introduce herself.

"Hey, I'm Kristen." She pauses and awkwardly waves at the group before dropping her hand back in her lap. "Uh… I'm a baker, but have a full culinary background and haven't always just baked. The last thing I remember was a man walking up to me as I left the Fleetwood Mac concert. Told me he was having car trouble and asked if I'd help him with a jump start. I agreed and drove my car over to where he said his was, about a hundred feet away. Last I remember, I was opening the trunk to get my jumper cables. And then nothing."

"Where was your concert at?" Billie studied Kristen, trying to find a link that their captor said they wouldn't.

"Just outside Richmond. Why?"

Billie shook her head. "Nothing. Just wondering if it was near any of us. Hadn't heard Fleetwood Mac was touring, but sometimes I'm out of the loop with concerts and events."

Waiting for everyone to quiet, the last woman—the pecan-brown haired woman—introduced herself. Her voice timid and small, causing everyone to lean forward.

"My name's Nina. I'm a schoolteacher. Was driving home from an out-of-town trip to see my daughter. On my way back, my car started acting crazy. All the lights on the dashboard lit up. I pulled over and called roadside assistance. When the man arrived, he started looking under the hood. Pointing to components of the engine near the dash. I leaned in to see what he was pointing at and that's the last thing I remember."

The group fell silent. Everyone introspective about their own circumstances and thinking how the other six landed here. Their faces disheveled like a mountain of puzzle pieces as they each worked to connect the small shapes and create the big picture. Determine what motive brought them to this place.

Minutes ticked by before the silence was interrupted. A plan enacted.

"Well, ladies. You ready for your knight in shining armor to break you out of this dungeon?" Skip planted his hands on the grimy armrests of the chair he'd been sitting in and stood, the legs scraping the wood and creating a nails-on-the-chalkboard effect.

Kelly smirked before answering his knightly question. "Yeah, Skip. Let me know when he gets here." A round of female laughter echoed throughout the sparse, musty room. Skip sneered, spun on his heel, and stormed out of the room.

CHAPTER TWO

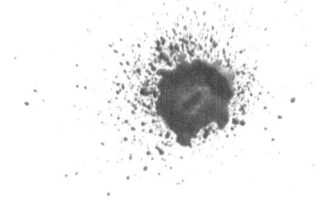

SKIP STORMED off from the throng of women. Their laughter at his previous comment reddened his face and pissed him off. Past the couch, he entered a large space occupied by a dusty, wooden dining table—three chairs parked on either side of the long edge and one at each end.

Cleaned up, this dining set would look nice in any home, Skip thought.

Off to the left of the dining room was a foyer. The narrow space held a single piece of furniture—a small side table beside the front door. Cobwebs trailed from an ornamental bowl on the table to an adjacent window. The bowl blanketed in a heavy layer of dust. Pieces of filthy artificial fruit rested in its goblet.

Stepping closer to the door, Skip reached for the handle and twisted the knob. He needed to satisfy his curiosity after reading the letter. In the letter, their captor stated he would let them leave once his sick and twisted fantasy got fulfilled. But Skip's stubbornness had to at least give leaving a valiant effort.

Inspecting the door closer, Skip noticed more than one

type of lock. The lock attached to the door handle had a large display with a numerical keypad and five buttons exhibiting random symbols. Above the keypad was two heavy-duty deadbolts with separate touch screen displays. He had seen these before—fingerprint scanning locks—and they were hardcore and foolproof.

"Well, this is just *fantastic*." Skip rolled his eyes and shook his head. "I could try to figure out the code to the keypad, but that could take days. Or we can search the house for tools. Anything I can break the locks with."

The cluster of women spun to face the door. Their eyes trained on Skip's every move. Billie jumped at the opportunity to help Skip find whatever tools he required. Kelly laughed uncontrollably. The other four women stood rooted in place, unsure of what to do next.

"What's so funny?" Skip sneered and rested a hand on the back side of his hip. The round curve of his beer-belly protruded outward further and gave him the curvature of a pregnant woman. Kelly doubled over in laughter—eyes watering, nose dripping.

When she could finally speak, Kelly wiped the fallen tears from her cheeks. "So, *Mr. Saves The Day*, who also happens to be a locksmith… can't get the locks open, huh? Glad this isn't a life or death situation. Makes me wonder if you have trouble with other… *things* as well."

Skip gazed at each of the women as they stood silent and waited for his reaction. Each of them restrained their obvious desire to snicker at his expense. But they would burst any moment. All but one. She seemed torn. Both disappointed and amused. Billie. She ogled over him.

Ready and eager to do whatever Skip asked of her. He gave her a quick smile and winked, delighted she would slowly fall under his spell.

"I am a locksmith… of normal locks. These locks here" —Skip motioned to the bolts on the painted metal door— "these are some kind of military-grade, secret ops bullshit. Whoever put us here isn't just crazy. They're smart and have major connections. Consumers can't just buy this shit."

He pinned a stern gaze on Kelly, smirking and wanting to rub his knowledge in her face. Her mouth flattened in a straight line as irritation colored her cheeks.

"Whatever, man. What should we be looking for to bust the locks?" Kelly asked, annoyance lacing her tone.

Skip gazed from one woman to the next. Each of them masked with a blank stare. True, each of these women was gifted in their own way. But it was obvious none of them knew much about breaking and entering. In this particular situation, it should be referenced as breaking and exiting.

Picking up on how they needed guidance from him, Kelly tossed out ideas like free money since Skip forgot his words.

"Okay, let's start with some basics. Everyone, search wherever you can. See if you can find any tools—a hammer, screwdriver, and so on. Or anything similar in nature. Whatever you find, bring it to the dining table and we'll see what we can do with it. Go!"

Everyone headed in different directions in search of an implement. Anything that might help them escape. Billie went back to the living room, stood in the center, and spun in slow circles while her eyes scanned every surface. Along the farthest wall, a glass-door armoire sat loaded with books and baskets and various knickknacks. A cloudy film coated the glass, but not enough to block out the contents. On the two other walls, Billie scanned smaller shelving units. Each overflowed with children's toys, framed photographs, and a few pieces of sculpted art.

Billie stepped closer to one of the shelving units. Leaning in, she studied one of the framed photographs. The photo paper yellowed around the edges of the black and white portrait. A dark-haired woman sat in a wingback chair in a dress circa late-1800s, early-1900s. She sat tall with not a single hair out of place. Her demeanor oozed power. Beside her was a man. Standing tall at her side, he rested a hand on her shoulder. His aura wasn't as domineering as the woman, but authority dripped from his features. Billie picked up the picture. "So odd," she mumbled. "Wonder who they are."

Setting the picture down, she stepped closer to the small sculptures. Her hands slipped around the statuesque bust of a man. A man who resembled the one in the photo. A thin film coated her hands as she picked it up off the shelf. The weight tugged at her shoulders and she staggered backward. After she regained her balance, she rolled her shoulders to relax the working muscles. With the bust secured in her grasp, she scanned the other items on the shelves. Nothing notable sparked her interest, so she headed for the dining table.

Billie set the bust on the table with a loud thump and rotated her shoulder joints a few times. She scanned the dining area for anything useful. Opposite the living room, she spotted Jennifer and Kristen in the kitchen. They went section by section through the open, vast space. One by one, they opened cabinet after cabinet.

Each of the cabinets was loaded with every possible item a kitchen needed. Plates and cups. Pots and pans. Baking sheets and casserole dishes. Food, food, and tons more food. The pantry supplied well enough to feed a dozen people for weeks. Stockpiled with a variety of canned meats, beans, vegetables and fruits, and every baking ingredient and dried version of perishable staples.

Utterly wonderful and disturbing at the same time.

Kristen stopped short. The cabinet in front of her open. Not a single inch of the cabinet bare. Packed as if the people living here wouldn't need to leave for months. "This kitchen has everything imaginable. And tons of it. Whoever brought us here... they either intend to keep us here a while. Or they're trying to fatten us up. Not sure which idea bothers me more," Kristen stated.

Jennifer glanced at Kristen with narrowed eyes. She shook her head ever so slightly before resuming her search. After what felt like hours of exploring the cabinets, they moved on to the long line of drawers.

Opening them one by one, Jennifer and Kristen slowly inched closer to each other at the center of the kitchen. When they both reached their final drawer simultaneously, Jennifer signaled for Kristen to open hers first.

Tugging on the handle—wood squealed against wood, the drawer complaining against the frame—the drawer slipped open. Inside was a surplus of kitchen cooking tools.

Jennifer's hand dove into the drawer and retrieved several of the implements.

Scattering them along the counter, Jennifer picked up a select few items. A roasting fork, the steel tines solid and roughly a half inch thick. A meat tenderizer, the dulled mallet a single, solid piece of metal—one side of the head flat, the other covered in a mass of sharp, pyramid-shaped tenderizers. And lastly, a bottle opener with a sharp curl on its end—intended for puncturing tin cans or bottle corks.

Jennifer glanced at Kristen as both of them smiled wide with their discoveries. "I think these might help. They're sort of like chisels and a hammer," Jennifer said with a shrug. "Maybe they can pry the locks off."

Kristen nodded. "Let's bring them to the table and then see if we can help anyone else."

They grabbed their winnings and headed out of the kitchen. Stepping around the kitchen island that also doubled as a half-wall, they ambled into the dining room with a look of victory on their faces.

"Hey, Billie. What'd you find?" Jennifer prompted as she set the kitchen tools down on the filth-coated wood.

"I found this statue head thingy." Billie pointed to the grimy bust sitting at one end of the table. "It's heavy. I thought maybe we could use it to maybe bust one of the locks or something."

"Cool. We found these." Jennifer waved a hand over the three tools she and Kristen discovered in the kitchen. "Anyone else come back yet?"

"No. I wasn't sure if I should go look in another room or

not. So, I just stayed here and waited for someone else to join me."

Jennifer nodded. "Well, let's go see where everyone else is. Maybe we can help them and speed this up."

The three women ambled out of the dining room and made a beeline to the hallway. Booms and clacks erupted. The wood floor vibrated occasionally. The inherent sounds of destruction grew louder as they stepped closer to the first bedroom—the room where Kelly and Billie originally found Skip, Kristen, and Nina.

Jennifer reluctantly peeked around the doorframe to figure out what—or who—caused all the ruckus. Clothing and blankets and pillows flew in the air across the room. Jennifer startled back for a split-second. Belinda stood in the far corner, curled in on herself, while Skip threw everything unusable his hands touched across the room.

After a minute of witnessing the chaos, Jennifer knocked on the doorframe. Skip stopped abruptly and directed his attention toward the door. "You guys need a hand? We've found all we can from the living room and kitchen."

A noticeable flush spread over Skip's face as his jaw ticked with irritation. "Sure. Not like *she's* any help." Skip pointed to the corner where Belinda tried to let the walls swallow her whole.

Agitation flared beneath Belinda's skin—her lips tightened and eyes narrowed as her face reddened like a ripe tomato. But her volume was the single thing that caught everyone off-guard. "Well… if I wasn't in the same room as some prick asshole—who thinks he knows everything—I would've found something by now. Instead, I have to stand in the corner because you're throwing shit around the room like a toddler with zero control. The destructive path you've created makes it a little difficult to look through other parts of the room, considering I have to practically clear a path to any place I want to look."

All eyes locked on to Belinda as she heaved against the wall. In the newfound silence, Belinda's constant inhalations were all anyone heard. After a minute, Jennifer bent at the waist as one arm clutched her stomach and the other slapped her knee. A voluminous laugh belted from her chest and shook the room. Seconds ticked by as her hysterics bounced off the faded paisley wallpaper and boosted Skip's irritation. When she stood upright again, tears stained her cheeks and pooled in her eyes.

"That was fucking great!"

Another bout of laughter floated in the air, this time it stemmed from every person in the room. Every person except for Skip.

The women all laughed at his expense. And he seethed for the one who sparked the idea. Jennifer. She made a mockery of him in front of everyone. Gave them the impression he was a fool. A moron. An imbecile. Never had he been so livid in his life. Nor would he allow this Skip bashing session to continue.

Grabbing the closest thing to him, he launched a book across the room toward Jennifer's face. She ducked her head out of the line of fire before the book made contact. "All of you! Get. The fuck. Out! I'll search the rest of this fucking room on my own. Don't need a single goddamn one of you!"

"Whatever, asshat. Ladies, let's go find Nina and Kelly." Jennifer spun on her heel and headed for the hall, Belinda and Kristen in her wake.

Billie stood at the door for a beat, watching Skip as he hurled item after item from inside a dresser drawer. The moth-eaten clothing whipping through the air and landing on the far side of the bed. "Sorry she laughed at you," Billie muttered.

Skip peered over his shoulder in Billie's direction—ready to respond—but she had already turned her back to him and headed out to the hall. He stared at the empty doorframe for a beat, waiting to see if she would return. When she didn't, he grabbed more clothes and flung them across the room.

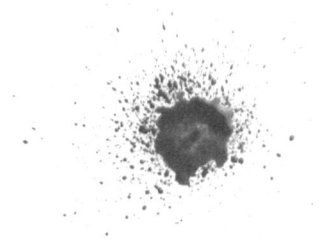

The seven gathered around the dining table and surveyed their newly discovered possessions. The mucky wooden surface displayed the miscellaneous discoveries like precious works of art. Marble bust from the living room. Roasting fork, meat tenderizer, and bottle opener from the kitchen. An old metal comb, pair of sewing shears, and a small stash of paperclips and bobby pins from the bedrooms. Was an odd combination of implements.

Almost feels like we're playing Clue, Nina thought. *It was the butler with the candlestick in the creepy doll room.*

They were hopeful and accepted the treasures as if they were gifts from the gods. But every few minutes, one of their faces donned a layer of disappointment.

"Well," Skip began. "Let's see what we can do with this stuff."

Reaching across the table, Skip picked up the roasting fork and meat mallet. He strutted out of the room and headed for the high-tech bolted door. His confidence decreased with each step forward, but he refused to be the butt of someone's joke again. He was a lady's man, after all.

Staring at the technology on the door, Skip knew it would be a huge feat busting the locks that held them captive. But he had zero plans on sharing that tidbit of information with a room full of people. Women, no less. Women who were a thorn in his side—except for one.

Placing the tines of the fork at the top edge of the number pad, Skip raised his other hand and slammed the flat side of the mallet against the butt of the fork. A loud, metal-on-metal, scraping pierced the air. The cluster of women slapped hands to their ears and squinted in pain.

Skip lifted the fork and mallet away to inspect the damage. As he suspected, the lock hadn't budged.

Lining the fork and mallet back up, Skip took another thwack at the lock. The mallet clanged against the butt again and another screech echoed in the narrow room, causing the ladies to step back. Inspecting it again, there was still no change with the lock. Although Skip knew busting these locks was damn near impossible, his frustration grew with each attempt. Hit after hit after hit. He refused to give up.

But after multiple failed attempts, Skip removed the roasting fork from the equation and repeatedly smashed the mallet against the keypad.

No change whatsoever. Not a scratch, nor a dent. No nicks. Not a single ding.

He paused—arms limp at his sides, left hip cocked out, eyes intently focused on the three menacing deterrents. Tilting his head right—eyes narrowed, forehead creased, lips pursed—Skip thought and thought of any other possible ways to manipulate the locks.

Turning back to the table, he tightly wrapped a hand around the bust statue and picked it up. He walked back to the door, studied it a moment, then took a step back and bashed the set of locks repeatedly with the bust.

The ripples of metal and stone colliding under the beat-down drove Skip forward, over and over again. A wicked grin stretched wider on his face with each strike. Victory soared in his chest with each thump of the bust against the locks.

Wanting to check the progress he'd made, Skip halted the battering session and inhaled deeply. After a step back, Skip stood more upright as his eyes scanned the bolts. A ghastly expression decorated the lines of his face. His jaw dropped.

How could this be? Skip thought.

His eyes drifted down to the bust still firmly gripped in his palm. Fragments of the torso were missing. Jagged edges stabbed out in anger. A long fracture splintered from the base to the neck of the bust. And a small trail of blood oozed down his hand toward his elbow.

When did I start bleeding?

Skip shook his head before it dropped in defeat. Failure flooded his veins like poison. "I think we can assume the locks aren't going anywhere. Think it's time for a plan B."

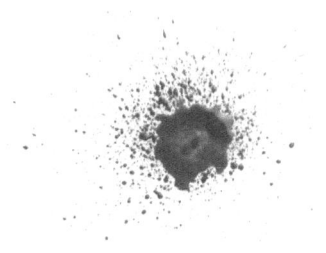

Everyone gathered in the living room. All seven sets of eyes glued to the wooden coffee table in front of the couch. The room eerie and still.

Kelly leaned forward, rested her elbows on her knees, laced her fingers while she spun her thumbs in circles. Billie peeked up from under her lashes and scanned the circle of faces before landing and staying on Skip's.

All of them blanketed in bewilderment. Unsure what to do next. And then it struck. A lightbulb lit above Belinda like a beacon of hope.

"I feel like we're all so stupid for not already thinking about this..." Everyone looked to Belinda. "We should check all the windows." She pointed at the large window on her left. Beneath the large pane sat one of several shelving units in the room.

Skip jumped to his feet. "Yes! Perfect idea. Okay everyone, split up. Pick a room, check all the windows and see if any of them will open. Let's go!" Skip clapped his hands.

Belinda threw Skip a snide smile before heading down the hallway, back to the bedroom she originally found herself in when she woke. Billie ambled over to the window in the living room. Kelly opted to check the bathroom window. Nina and Jennifer headed to the first bedroom. Meanwhile, Kristen strode into the kitchen, leaving Skip with the smaller windows in the foyer.

Clanks and grunts and groans ricocheted throughout the house. Quickly followed up with huffs and curses. One by one, each of them wandered back to the living room. A few of them plopped onto the couch and sent a cloud of dust into the air. Almost as quickly as the idea sparked, it extinguished. Within moments, all of them sat around the table again. Melancholy occupied the thick, dank air.

"Anything?" Kelly gazed up from her lap and waited to hear good news.

Like a wave in the stadium stands, each of them shook their heads. A few murmured *no's* disrupted the silence. The hope from moments ago had vanished.

"I found a door at the end of the hall, across from the back bedroom, that has bolts on it like the front door. I tried the handle, but nothing happened. So, I gave up and came back out here," Belinda stated.

This new information intrigued the group for a microsecond. The intrigue died as everyone recalled the failed attempts at breaking the locks on the front door. How on earth would they break the same type of locks on a different door? Simple. They wouldn't.

"Okay. Let's see if we can break any of them." Belinda threw out the idea. Once again, a dash of hope ignited within the group.

Rising from the couch, Kelly walked over to the dining table. Her hand hovered over the mallet and the bust. A few seconds of contemplation passed before she reached down and wrapped her fingers around the cold silver handle. Instead of heading for the hall, Kelly walked to one of the glass panes in the living room.

"Everyone stand back," Kelly announced.

Instantly, everyone leaped from their seats. Six sets of feet clacked against the floor as they shuffled back and lined up along the opposite wall. Kelly drew her hand back —as if preparing to launch a baseball to a batter—shielded her eyes in the crook of her left arm, and launched her right hand forward.

The mallet made contact with the window. A loud ringing filled the air and bounced off the walls, reverberating from the mallet in her hand and vibrating up her limb. Kelly lifted her arm away. Slowly, her eyes adjusted to the light and assessed the damage. Rooted in place, her mouth dropped open as her pupils dilated wider and wider.

"You have got to be fucking kidding me." Her words tumbled out in staccato. "What in the literal fuck. This is bullshit."

She reared her hand back once more, heaved it forward, and slammed the mallet against the pane again. And again. And again. The pane not giving way to even the slightest fracture or splinter.

She reached out and brushed her hand over the surface. The pane smooth to the touch—no grazing, no etching. Not even a visible ding. She continually ran her hand across the material—obviously not glass—trying to understand how it wouldn't give way.

"I think this is some sort of super thick, high-density polymer." Her eyes mesmerized as her hand slid side to side. But then she stopped. Barely noticeable, Kelly spotted something on the other side of the pane.

"What the hell does that mean?" Billie inquired, voice bubbly yet confused.

"It means that, by the looks of it, this window is a few inches thick and made of material, even at its thinnest state, is difficult to break. Whoever brought us here… we aren't leaving until they want us to. It also looks like there are bars on the outside of the window. I'm sure the other windows are identical."

A whimper from Billie broke the stunned silence. Everyone spun in place to face her. She caught everyone's stares with her whining as she tugged at the bottom hemline of her shirt.

"Does anyone have a cell phone on them?"

Each of them patted their pockets and came up empty-handed. Belinda scanned the room. "Anyone seen a purse lying around? I stash my phone there most of the time."

"I don't remember seeing any purses anywhere," Kelly answered. "While we searched the house, anyone remember seeing a landline?"

A universal *no* resounded from everyone's lips. The temperament in the room shifted to doom and gloom. Hope took a step back while fear simmered in the periphery. Seven minds diligently working to come up with new ways to leave the filth-hole they sat in.

Lost in their own headspace, none of the seven heard the first click in the hallway. The second and third click echoed louder. The sounds easily bounced down the corridor and out into the silence consuming them. Jennifer raised her head first, checking to see if anyone else heard the noises.

"Did you hear that?" Jennifer asked, her voice coated in the dust particles floating through the air.

"Hear what?" Skip stared at her with a furrowed brow.

Wood creaked in the hall and everyone's head perked up. Eyes instantly veered in the direction of the sound. Skip bolted up from his seat. *Thump. Thump. Thump.* His shoes pounded against the hardwood as he made his way to the hallway. The closer he got to the source, the louder and faster the sound moved. As soon as he rounded the corner, the door at the end slammed shut.

Thwack. Thwack. Clunk.

Standing at the start of the hall, he stared at the door for a long moment and said nothing. His eyes drifted down to the floor, landed on the wood in front of the bolted door, and noticed a new envelope. Skip dashed the short distance down the corridor, bent to grab the envelope and returned to the others.

"What the hell just happened?" Kelly asked as soon as Skip sat back down.

He stared at the envelope in his hand a moment longer before lifting his head to look everyone in the eyes. "The door at the end of the hall... it opened. Someone unlocked the door, set this on the floor, then closed and bolted the door shut again." He held the envelope up for everyone to see.

Kelly yanked the envelope from his hand, tore the flap open, and pulled out the paper inside. She scanned it for a second before reading it aloud to the group.

I thought I told you all to not attempt to leave. Thought I made myself clear. The only way you leave this house is when I decide. Do as I have instructed. If you try to escape again, you will regret your actions. Severely. You may not be swimming in the lap of luxury, but you have everything you need here to survive. Enjoy the break from your lives. Enjoy each other. When I am ready to bid you farewell, you will be the first to know. Till then...

D

"This sick freak wants us to pretend like we're at some sort of retreat?" Skip threw his hands up as his tone escalated with each word he spit out. "It'd be easier to pretend like we're on some getaway if we weren't in a shithole!"

The light in the room vanished. The empty space between the group black and unnatural. Mechanical noises crackled nearby. A few of the women startled and called out for help. Metal scraped against metal—sharp and fast. A moment later, blinding light brightened the room. Everyone slammed their eyes shut to subdue the sudden luminescence.

One by one, they opened their eyes and adjusted to the

transition from dark to light. A universal gasp erupted in the room.

What the hell was this place?

The living room morphed. Changed. Converted. As if the seven had been abducted from one house and put into another. But that wasn't possible. Neither was a house which could alter its appearance in seconds or minutes. Absent was the grimy sheen on all the furniture. Not a speck of dust in sight. The walls garnered a fresh coat of paint rather than the peeling wallpaper. Even the furniture was different—modern and clean. Every surface immaculate. Every inch of fabric impeccable. The musty mildew stench less noticeable.

Jennifer ran a hand over the blue couch. The soft fabric flexed under her touch. Trying to grasp what just happened, Jennifer spoke what entered everyone's mind. "I'm so confused... where the hell are we? Is this some kind of sick and twisted experiment?"

CHAPTER THREE

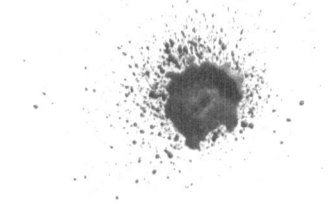

HOVERED around the coffee table for more than an hour, the group quietly discussed what they each remembered. With each new story, they worked like detectives to solve the mystery that was the house which they currently resided. In the blink of an eye, every lick of the structure morphed into something new.

Billie suggested it was all a nightmare. But the moment the words left her tongue, the others rebutted. The concept great, but how could they all be in the same nightmare? None of them knew each other. As far as they were concerned, none of them lived or worked within a ten-mile radius. Hence, the nightmare concept was squashed.

Jennifer proposed maybe they were all in a room together. Knocked out and connected through some mind-meld. Playing someone's twisted version of a game. The group granted Jennifer's scenario more plausibility before shoving it to the wayside. Her *Matrix*-like philosophy wasn't too far-fetched in the day and age of virtual reality. How else could walls and furniture change instantaneously?

Questions and ideas were thrown around for minutes comparable to hours. Who did this? Why? What does he or she have to gain by holding people hostage? What will happen to each of them? Why them? Did they do something to deserve this? The questions kept coming. But every answer or solution the group came up with didn't stick.

Eventually the questions died down. The new atmosphere of the house more relaxing and visually stimulating. As the second hand ticked on, the group fell into a more comfortable silence. Lounging on the plush couches. Reading books from the now full shelves. Discovering complex puzzles to scatter across the dining table and distract their minds. Even getting to know one another a little bit better. The types of things people did prior to the invasion of technology.

Seven strangers had been thrown into a peculiar situation. Locked away in a strange house. But, slowly, their minds forgot the house surrounding them was a nightmare less than an hour prior. Perhaps the house was not the only thing altered when the blackness consumed their vision. Perhaps more was at play.

Jennifer, Kelly, and Nina scattered and sorted pieces of a puzzle across a glossy black dining table built for ten. The image on the puzzle box resembled that of a photograph versus a stock image—a tattered young woman walking down a path in the woods, the moon rising above the tree line of a starry sky. They sorted the pieces by color, setting aside any resembling the edge. Then they constructed the border. Once the border was complete, they each chose a section to work on and chatted with one another. Smiles and laughter commenced as the women became familiar with one another.

"So, do either of you have anyone at home that'll be wondering where you are?" Jennifer asked as she tried to fit a piece into the border corner.

"I don't," Kelly answered. "I had a roommate a couple of months ago, but she moved in with her girlfriend. Haven't been able to find anyone else, yet."

Nina nodded. "I have no one at home, either. I was leaving my daughter's house and heading home. She might get concerned when I don't check in and let her know I got home safe. But, oftentimes, she gets bogged down with work and doesn't think about checking in."

"What about her father?" Jennifer asked.

"He passed away a few years ago. Congestive heart failure finally took its toll on him."

"Sorry to hear that."

"Thank you. So, what about you?"

"Nope. No roommates. No boyfriend or girlfriend. Just me. My job doesn't really give me much time to do anything aside from sleep—and sometimes sleep is sparse. It's okay, though. Eventually, one day, I'll find the one, *right*?"

Kelly and Nina nodded as they tried to fit different pieces into their section of the puzzle. The weight of Jennifer's last statement resonated with them. Made them question the life they lived. Their solitude.

Trying to lighten the sudden heavy mood, Kelly pointed over to Billie and Skip. Jennifer, Kelly, and Nina watched the couple with curious eyes. A sense of wonder flooded their heads. A wonder of which direction that story headed.

"I don't get it," Nina said. "What exactly does she find appealing?" Jennifer and Kelly shrugged; eyes still glued to the now laughing duo.

"Not sure. Maybe she's had trouble finding *the one*," Kelly suggested. "To each their own, I suppose."

Billie gravitated toward Skip from the moment she laid eyes on him. Skip openly admitted to being a sex fiend and dated anyone willing. Dating for him was strictly to have sex. The two of them sat on a cushy loveseat—the one which magically appeared when the house shifted—and whispered to each other. Billie quite animated when she spoke—her mouth in a constant smile as her hands spoke a language all their own.

On the full-length couch, Belinda stretched out her legs with a book in her hands. The book cover resembled a photograph—like the puzzle box. A young woman in a field of tall grass and wildflowers, her hands skimming the surface as she walked toward a historic, white two-story home with the sun setting in the backdrop. Judging by the number of pages, the book quite lengthy—easily four- to five-hundred pages thick. At this point, Belinda already made a sizable dent reading the story.

Kristen traipsed off to the kitchen—opening and closing every cabinet and drawer. She scoured the fridge and discovered it had been filled with new items. Kristen floated through the kitchen like a ballerina on stage. Anyone watching her would instantly realize Kristen loved being in a kitchen. Loved the endless gadgets and gizmos.

Loved whipping ingredients together and serving food to others.

One by one, Kristen removed boxes and cans from the cabinets. She stared at the packaging, turning them over a time or two. Obviously unfamiliar with some of the brands or products. Carefully, she read each package and deciphered its contents. Each time she finished, a small *hmm* exited her lips.

As if a lightbulb flickered over her head, she snagged pen and paper from one of the drawers. One at a time, she listed each item she pulled from the cabinets and created an inventory list. An aid which helped her figure out what to cook everyone later.

Seven strangers under one roof felt less unfamiliar now. By no means were they best buds. But in a few short hours, seven people settled into their new surroundings with almost unheard-of ease. They each found ways to smile or laugh or be comfortable. The new interior proved their current predicament to be less unfavorable. Who wouldn't love time off from their monotonous life?

Soon they wouldn't feel trapped inside the house. Wouldn't think of each other as strangers. Eventually, they would lower their walls and form a sense of trust. A trust seven strangers shouldn't exchange.

Because the one question left unanswered was who brought them here. Who trapped seven strangers in a house for the unforeseeable future?

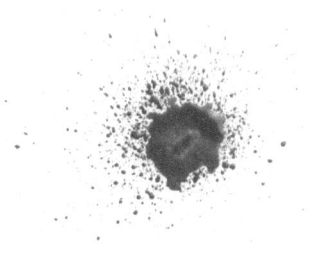

SKIP

This blonde has given me a raging hard-on since the moment I laid eyes on her. My fucking pants have constricted my favorite body part for hours. Little Skippy is throbbing like a son of a bitch—dying to come out and play. I reach down and adjust my cock for the umpteenth time, not giving a shit if she or anyone else notices.

She rambles on incessantly. Constantly talking. Words flowing out of her mouth as rapid as the Rio Grande. I have yet to determine if her chatter is cute or annoying. Only time will tell.

On occasion, I hear a word or two. Kind of hard to keep up when she talks a million miles per hour. But I remember to nod every once in a while. Women like that. Acknowledgment. And over the years, I have mastered said skill without truly having to listen. Call it a gift.

If I have to be stuck in this weird-ass house—which by some fucking miracle revamped from a negative-star shithole into a five-star lap of luxury—at least one of these women isn't cold as ice.

And the way she ogles over me… I adjust myself again.

Maybe I will score a chance with this one. Honestly, she seems interested in me. The last thing I want to do is fuck over whatever luck has been thrown my way. So, I best act as if I give a shit about something other than getting my rocks off. After all, I'm not completely heartless.

She finishes talking about whatever kept her lips flapping for the last five minutes—something about a couple who visited the diner she works at—and looks to me for a response. Not sure what I missed during my introspection, so I shoot for vague and hope it fits.

"Really?"

I hope to fucking Christ my response is suitable. Can't have this one upset with me. She is the only one here who stares at me with doe eyes. Doe eyes I picture watering as I shove my cock down her throat.

"I know, right? Thought it was kinda crazy the old man had a girl young enough to be his granddaughter with him as a date. Gross." She visibly shivers in front of me. Her body attempting to shake the thought away.

I inwardly cringe. Not hours before, I told everyone I'd been on a date with a twenty-year-old and how I was twenty-seven years her senior. Would Billie be turned off because of that? I sure as hell hope not. Too many days have passed since my last lay and I am edging. Desperation is a needy bitch and she is slowly slithering up my spine. The more interested she seems, the harder my dick gets. And the more uncomfortable I get. My zipper painfully grinds against my erection.

So, I need to test the water. See if this whole charade is a waste of my time. Not to be an asshole—nature of the beast

—but I don't want to spend precious minutes trying to woo this one if it won't pan out.

"So, what kind of guys do you normally date?" I ask.

She toys with the ends of her shoulder-length strands, twirling them around her fingertips. Her eyes dart around the room, looking everywhere except at me. Is she scared to tell me? She's been a never-ending stream of chitchat for what feels like hours.

"Um… I don't know. Guess I like older guys, but not old enough to be my grandfather, obviously." She laughs, but it's more out of nerves than hilarity. "Most have brown hair. Don't really know. Don't pay enough attention to details, I suppose. If they enjoy having a good time and find me attractive, I guess that's all that matters."

I have never been happier to listen to a woman speak. Her words are music to my ears. Everything leaving her lips is reassurance I have a chance with her. She doesn't seem too invested in love or the sappy bullshit. Bonus!

Another telltale sign… she has followed me around like a lost puppy since she laid eyes on me. If I can't sweet-talk this one into sex, I take full credit for losing my A-game. Because scoring with her should be a slam dunk.

"It's okay. Not everyone has a set-in-stone type they look for. I don't." Reaching over, I tuck a few wayward strands of her blonde hair behind her ear, brushing my fingertips against her soft skin in the process. A soft smile brightens her face as her eyes flicker to mine. A light blush pinks her skin and I mentally place a checkmark in the WIN column.

This may be easier than originally anticipated.

Some guys are ass men. Others have a thing for a pair of firm tits. Me? I truly have no preference. Sure, I love a tight ass and full, perky tits. Anyone who loved women would be an idiot not to. But as long as the women I engaged with were into men, I gave two shits about their appearance. Beauty is simply a blessing. Maybe they wouldn't have to be face down.

Hell, even if the women who captivated me weren't into guys, I'd ask to watch. Get off on the whole visual. What red-blooded man wouldn't? As long as the end result happened, I was satisfied.

"So, *Billie*, what do you like to do for fun?"

If my plan was to get this woman beneath me, I had to put on a show. Make her believe I was interested in her as a person to some degree. As much as I hated small talk, it was essential in certain situations.

"If I had to choose only one thing…" She taps a finger against her lips as she thinks. My cock flinches at the sight. "Hands down, I'd say karaoke. I'm kind of a legend at Player's Bar and Grill. Ever been there?"

"Can't say I have. If you're as legendary as you say you are, I'd never forget you. What kind of music do you sing to?"

A flush blooms over her cheeks as she sits up straighter. Her hands animate in front of her as she shares her love for singing other people's songs to strangers.

"I love, love, love P!nk. Could sing her songs all night long. Actually, one night at the bar, when no one else wanted to sing, I did. Stayed up on the stage for three or four hours and sang my heart out. Everyone kept

applauding me, so I figured why not carry on. Anyway…
besides her, I guess I'd say pop music is my go-to. Anything
with a catchy beat that's easy to sing along with."

Love how this chick is so easy to please. I could say
anything to her and she would be happy, simply because I
focused on her. It didn't seem to take much to impress her
—another tick mark in my favor. I wonder how much
longer I needed to drag this conversation on. How long
before I hinted at my desire to take her to one of the
bedrooms and fuck her brains out.

Her body language led me to believe she enjoyed every
ounce of attention I doled her way. From the blush in her
cheeks to the way her body inched a little closer to mine.
Over the years, I have mastered the art of reading body
language. Plus, she continually prattles on with conversation. Conversation mostly one-sided. But filling our time
with mindless chitchat is what she appears to enjoy. So, I
concede to the notion. A man has to take matters into his
own hands to get the job done. Am I right? Of course.

"That's cool. I don't really listen to one type of music. I
listen to a little bit of everything as long as it doesn't sound
like shit. Though, I'm sure everyone at Player's loves
listening to you sing. I know I'd sit there and listen to you
sing all night. Surely, a beautiful woman such as yourself
must have a beautiful voice."

A fresh smattering of crimson spreads over her face and
down along her chest. Is she so easily flattered? The compli-
ments strike her more when it is only the two of us. The
group hinders her response to me. I make a mental note of
this.

"You're just saying that to be nice." She playfully slaps at my arm. "I doubt anyone wants to listen to my squeaky voice all night. I've seen several people leave when they see me head for the small square the bar calls a stage. But I don't care. Plus… if the bar hasn't kicked me out yet, I must not be scaring off too many people. Right?"

In this exact moment, I wish there was some sort of karaoke machine in this house. Then I could really lay the charm on. I'd get up and sing with her. Embarrass the hell out of myself. Because my efforts would be rewarded with sex. And sex is always the endgame.

"Too bad there's no way to sing karaoke now. I'd sing with you. Would be fun."

Her eyes grow big, her smile bright and wide. *"You would? Really?"* She covers her mouth with her hand briefly. The minor gesture change catches me off guard and I lose focus. She notices me staring at her mouth and starts waving a hand in front of my face.

"Sorry. Didn't mean to stare. It's just…" I pause, contemplating how to say what I'm thinking.

"It's just what?"

"I really like you, Billie. You're so pretty. Prettier than any other woman I've met." I trace a fingertip down her bicep. "And a moment ago, when you touched your lips, I thought about kissing you."

Fuck my life.

Her hand lifts to her lips again—fingertips skimming over the plump, pink pillows I want wrapped around my cock. My balls tighten and scream for release. As quickly as she stroked her lips, her hand dropped to her lap. Her eyes dart to the rest of the group. She eyes them to see if they are paying us any attention. To see if they heard any part of our conversation.

The desperate side of me wants her out of their sight. Wants to find a bed—one a lot less disgusting than the one I woke up on earlier—and let loose on this willing blonde. Every inch of my skin prickles with anticipation. She seems eager, perhaps for different reasons than me. And her desire for me is all that matters.

She studies me momentarily. Thoughts on the tip of her tongue, but her voice isn't working. Three times now, her lips have parted to speak. And all three times, she's clamped them shut and not said a word. If she wasn't initiating, I would.

Getting a woman to the bedroom… let's just say I knew a thing or two about making this happen. Wouldn't call myself a master, but I have some damn fine skills. If men received merit badges or martial arts belts in womanizing, I would hold top honors.

"You want to look around the rest of the house and see what else has magically transformed?" A vague enough question. It doesn't insinuate any specific idea except to appease curiosity. But my mind—and dick—screams to find a bed. Now.

"Sure. Who knows what we'll find. This place is super weird. But at least it's clean now."

Victory.

"True."

Scooting forward, I rise from the love seat and extend my hand to her. She slips it easily into mine as she stands.

Five glaring sets of eyes are suddenly way more interested in our every movement. Ignoring their judgmental scowls, we step around the coffee table—now a white-painted wood number—and head toward the dining area and the hallway past it.

"Where you guys going?" Kelly chimes in with her irritating voice. It crawls across my skin and pisses me off.

Nosey bitch. Why the hell does she need to know where we're going? Or what we're doing? *Mind your own fucking business.*

"We're going to check out the rest of the house. See what else has changed." I wave my hand in the air. "After this *fabulous* makeover, who knows what else we're missing out on."

As we walk past the dining table—where Kelly, Jennifer, and Nina are currently trying to piece together some stupid looking puzzle—I glimpse Kelly rolling her eyes in my periphery.

Stupid bitch. Seriously, mind your own business.

As we wander down the hall, Billie turns left, heads into the bathroom, and drops my hand. "Be back in a minute."

After she shuts the door, I glance down the hall. The walls are now littered with various framed photos. Each image the size of a music poster. I amble over to the first one beside the first bedroom doorway. The closer I get, the more I try to decipher what exactly the photo is in the dim lighting.

Looks like a woman—her eyes covered with something dark, body splayed across a metal-looking gurney, arms pinned at her sides. I step back from the grotesque image. I may be into some twisted shit here and there, but this is a bit excessive. And it's an odd addition to the new "renovation" in the house. Everything else in the newer version of the house has been sophisticated and pristine. This does not fit the same modus operandi. I face away from it and hope to mask the image when Billie opens the bathroom door.

It works.

When Billie opens the door, she glances at me and then down the length of the hall. The first bedroom is feet away. She exits the bathroom, takes my hand, and walks us into the room.

The room has gotten a makeover like the main rooms of the house. Only one thing didn't change. The wall of shelves loaded with creepy dolls. She walks ahead of me and goes over to the dresser. She picks up a picture frame, studies it briefly, and sets it down before picking up another. My stomach knots at the possible photos. Are they similar to the one I found in the hall?

She continues the process. Sets one down. Picks up another. And doesn't say a single word. She studies the newest picture more closely. Her head cocks to the side. Something about it has piqued her curiosity—which now has me curious. I walk up behind her and peer over her shoulder at the vintage, gold-framed photograph.

In the photo, the lighting is low. The woman blends into the background and it's difficult to differentiate her from her surroundings. Billie brings the picture closer and studies the woman with immense interest. From my position behind her, I note the edges of the woman's blonde strands. In the photo, the woman appears to be laying down. Her face in partial profile.

Recognition strikes me like a bat to the skull. I know her. The woman in the photo. Sucking in a deep breath, I refuse to exhale until the burn in my lungs becomes unbearable. Watching over Billie's shoulder, I study her expression out of the corner of my eye. She hasn't put two-and-two together yet. Not sure if I should be relieved or concerned.

One can only hope she doesn't figure it out.

Pleasure washes over me as I watch her set the frame back on the dresser. Assuming she did not recognize her own image in the photo, I take her hand and drag her away from possibly picking up the picture again.

"Hey, let's go check out the other room. This wall of dolls is freaking me the fuck out. Not sure how you feel about them, but I'm not a fan."

She nods, and I'm grateful she accepted my reason to leave. Her hand encased in mine, we exit the room and go farther down the hall. One more door on the right is the only other viable option. As we enter the room, I glance over my shoulder at the door with three high-tech locks resting along the right center across the hall.

Is the sick fuck who brought us here just on the other side? If he is, I hope I get my hands on him. Fucking asshole.

Once I take in the second bedroom, I sigh in relief. This bedroom is much more pleasant on the eyes. The first thing I notice is the lack of porcelain, lifelike dolls. *Thank fuck.* Those fuckers gave me the heebie-jeebies. The second thing I notice is the massive bed butted against the far wall.

Fuck yes.

Four large, wooden posts stand erect at each corner of the bed. At the top of each post, a beam extends to the next post—all four posts connected by a second frame near the ceiling. Sheer fabric bunches at each post. If let loose, the fabric would enclose whoever was on the bed and shut out the surrounding room. Billie probably finds it romantic. But romance isn't my forte.

The idea of fucking Billie on this bed has my dick hard as stone. I drop a hand to my groin and adjust myself—for the millionth time—as my erection becomes beyond uncomfortable in my briefs. If I don't get relief soon, my balls will shrivel up, turn to raisins, and fall off.

I watch her walk around the room—as she did in the last room—and catch her picking up various objects. A gold necklace with a green stone at the heart. A silver filigree bracelet. An antique, ornate comb. The room cluttered with random keepsakes. No rhyme or reason to any of them. None of them pairs with anything else. Like someone went to an estate sale and purchased a load of miscellaneous knickknacks.

She traces her fingers along the surface of the dresser. A large mirror attaches at the back edge and displays the opposite side of her face. Her hand skims every nearby surface as if it could discover answers in the textures.

"Who do you think all this jewelry belongs to? And the photos... who do you think those people are?" Curiosity coats her words.

I have ideas about every item in this house—with the exception of the furniture. My opinion... the photos are of all the women this psychopath has abducted. As far as the jewelry is concerned, they might be random knickknacks. Or tokens. Personal items the abducted women had when they were taken. I think this house isn't only just a place for us to be held captive, but also a trophy room to showcase every person captured.

Am I going to tell her that? Hell fucking no, I'm not. If I share my theory, she'll run from the room screaming. Run to the five other women for comfort. So I play it off with a shrug. What can I say? I'm a selfish bastard.

"I have no idea. Maybe they're family members of whoever's house this is."

She studies me, unsure if she believes the spiel I deliver. I need to get her back to where we were earlier, out in the living room. I need her to stop thinking so much. If she continues down this path of questioning, I may never get what I need out of her. There is only one thing I want her focusing on. Me.

And right now... I really fucking need her. Only she can relieve the ache building inside me.

I walk over to her, grab her hand and encase it in both of mine.

"Hey. You shouldn't worry about such things. We just need to ride out this crazy lunatic's fantasy and then we'll be out of here. Okay?"

Bringing my hand to her chin, I tip her head back and lock eyes with her. She scrutinizes me a moment, eyes darting back and forth before her shoulders drop and her body sags against mine.

"Okay. I'll try. I just hate this. Who the hell does this kind of stuff? Who even thinks of it? It's so freaking crazy.

Never, in a million years, did I ever think something like this would happen to me. Never."

"Me either. Let's just make the best of it. All we can do is stay optimistic and not try to figure out why this guy is a nutbag." I lean forward and brush her lips with mine, testing the water.

Upon first touch, her lips don't respond to mine. I pull away, doubt filtering in and disappointment flooding my veins. I really thought I was going to get lucky with this one. Of all the women I'm stuck with in this insane situation, Billie is the only one who I have a chance with. The others are too smart for my old-school tricks.

But Billie... she has been fawning over me. Subliminally begging for my attention. As soon as I gave her attention, she bloomed before my eyes. Was so responsive to every line I delivered. From the heat blanketing her cheeks to her noticeable lean in my direction, I thought she wanted more. But now...

"I'm sorry. I thought you wanted... it seemed like you were open to... sorry."

Perhaps I read the signals all wrong. I have never misinterpreted the signals before. And right now, I am so fucking confused. How could I misconstrue our connection?

Her warm, nimble fingers graze the center of my chest. "You don't need to apologize. It's just that... I wasn't expecting that right then. It was nice."

It was nice. Does her sentiment mean she's open to the idea? God, I fucking hope so. I need answers. I need for this —us—to happen. Desperately.

I lean forward again and drop my mouth to hers,

pressing a short peck on her sweet lips. When I back off, she makes a move and initiates the second kiss. This one packed with more of a punch than its predecessor.

Time skirts by as we tease each other slowly with lips and hands. Still standing in the center of the room, I plot my path to get her to the bed. Heat things up. Take it up another notch. Just as I'm ready to move us closer to the bed, the tip of her tongue sweeps across my lower lip.

I don't move as a growl rips from my throat and my hands clutch her hips. Locking her in place, I grind my cock against her. I break the kiss and open my eyes. Billie stares back at me—pupils dilated and a foreign hunger vibrating off her. No doubt, she *feels* how rock hard I am. Now she senses how badly I need to fuck her, here and now.

She inches away slightly, and the loss has my body screaming for her return. Before I haul her front to mine, she wraps her dainty fingers around my erection. I throw my head back and hiss.

This cat and mouse game needs to end now. Taking ownership, I walk us toward the bed. Dropping my mouth to her skin, I kiss along her neck and suck the spot below her ear. Hope the rest of her tastes as sweet as this. Just the idea of tasting all of her has my dick in a frenzy.

I need her on this bed.

Need to see her bare flesh.

Need to trace every inch of her body with my fingers.

Need her warmth wrapped around my dick.

Need her lips on my cock.

Need to fuck her senseless.

I slip my hands under her arms, lift her off the floor, and

toss her on the bed. She laughs and positions herself like a 1950s pinup girl. Completely fucking adorable. But I didn't give a fuck how she sprawled across the bed. Only one thing mattered. Ripping off her clothes and exposing her naked flesh. And her hot, pink pussy.

As if reading my mind, she props herself up. On her knees, she sits back on her haunches. Attempting to look sexy. Her fingers dance along her shirt hem and tease me in slow motion. But it isn't long before she shifts gears. Not long before she grabs a fistful of material in her hands. She lifts the shirt over her head and reveals the start of what I know will be exactly what I need.

CHAPTER FOUR

KRISTEN WANDERED out of the kitchen, a legal pad in one hand and a pen in the other. She scanned down the long inventory list she scribbled on the paper. Strolling past the three at the dining table, she went into the living room and sat on the loveseat previously occupied by Skip and Billie.

Flipping the top page up, she noted the lengthy inventory. If the group had no idea how long they'd be at the house, and food needed to be rationed for their survival, Kristen felt obligated with the task. To plan meals with all the items she inventoried. To distribute them evenly and without favoritism. With her culinary background, she assumed the task and was eager to organize.

She tore the top two pages from the pad, set them aside, and let her mind wander. Eyes glazed over, she envisioned a list of meals to create. As ideas popped into her head, she jotted them onto a fresh page. She scanned the list of perishables as one recipe after another flew out of her internal recipe bank. The cabinets overflowed with possibilities and Kristen was just beginning to get them written down.

Kristen sat on the loveseat, scribbling furiously, with a

smile plastered across her face. Out of the corner of her eye, Kelly detected Kristen's exuberance. Kelly halted her puzzling, cocked her head, and observed Kristen. *Odd,* she thought.

Voice low, Kelly pointed toward Kristen with a puzzle piece still in her hand. "What do you think she's so excited about?"

Jennifer and Nina stopped searching through the puzzle piece mountain and followed Kelly's line of sight. The trio stood around the dining table and stared at Kristen as she smiled brighter with each scrawl on the pad of paper.

What the hell could be so wonderful about being stuck in this place, Kelly thought.

Jennifer shrugged and pursed her lips. "Don't know. She did say she was a cook or something. She *did* just walk out of the kitchen a minute ago. Maybe she's doing foodie stuff. Probably gets off on it." She shrugged again, then shifted her focus back to the puzzle for a moment, fist pumping when she fit a piece in place.

"Why don't you just ask her?" Nina proposed. "We could sit here and keep guessing. But guessing won't result in actual answers."

Kelly and Jennifer nodded at Nina's statement. Kelly glanced down at the table and shoved a puzzle piece she'd been holding a while into its potential place. Nope. She tossed it back into the pile and picked up another.

"Suppose I'll ask in a few. This puzzle is a pain in my ass. Is it too much to ask to place more than three pieces where they belong?" Kelly asked, frustration owning her words.

Spreading the unplaced pieces out on the table, Jennifer, Nina, and Kelly focused on the puzzle once again. Determination must have been on their side because the outline of a red-headed woman sitting poolside with a frozen drink in her hand became discernible. The more they focused, the more pieces they fit into place. Soon, they would finish.

"Is it just me, or does this puzzle seem a little weird?" Jennifer prompted.

Kelly and Nina stopped, hands hovered over the puzzle, and stared at Jennifer in bewilderment.

"What do you mean weird? I've done plenty of puzzles before. Seems like any other, just a different image," Nina stated.

"That's what I mean. The image..." Jennifer trailed off.

"What? Don't like redheads?" Kelly teased.

"Has nothing to do with the color of the woman's hair. More like... I don't know. This picture feels amateur." Jennifer picked up the box and held up the front for both of them to see as she pointed at various parts of the image while she spoke. "Like here, in the foreground and a little on the edges. There is a blurriness. Maybe leaves. Like the person who took the picture was hiding behind a bush or something."

"Okay, when you say it like that, it's a little creepy. Didn't really look at it from that angle before." Kelly locked on to the image on the box, examining it harshly, and tried to see what she hadn't noticed previously.

"And the woman isn't posing for the photo. She isn't looking at whoever is behind the camera. She's looking off at the other people by the pool. Almost like this picture was taken by an admirer and turned into a puzzle," Jennifer added.

Nina and Kelly simultaneously threw down the pieces in their hands and lifted their hands from the table. Nina shoved her chair back, the legs scraping against the floor as everyone nearby stared her way.

"Okay, I'm officially done with this. Maybe the puzzle is some sort of *trophy* to whoever brought us here. Maybe they get kicks from knowing other people are putting it together." Nina noticeably shivered.

Jennifer and Kelly followed suit and pushed back from the table. They each stared down at the partially assembled puzzle that formed the image of a woman who'd been secretly photographed.

Kelly leaned forward and began tearing apart the semi-completed puzzle. Soon after, Nina and Jennifer joined in on the breakdown. The pieces quickly formed an anthill on the table before they raked them back into the box.

Jennifer took the tainted puzzle, all the pieces back in the cardboard packaging, and placed it on the shelf in the living room where it was first discovered. Then she strolled over to where Belinda and Kristen sat and parked herself on the couch beside Belinda. Nina and Kelly appeared a moment later and squeezed onto the couch and loveseat.

"You guys give up on the puzzle already? It's only been an hour or so since you started it," Belinda asked, peeking over the top of her book.

Jennifer scratched the back of her head and furrowed her brow. "Yeah. The image started creeping us out, so... no more puzzle for us. How's the book?"

Belinda dog-eared the page she was reading and closed the book, setting it on the table. "It's alright. Seems like a psychological thriller. I love reading, but don't think I've ever heard of this author." She picked the book back up and read the cover before setting it back down. "It's called Before the Sun Rises by D. Marxman. Ever heard of him? Or her?"

The group shook their heads, each looking to the other for a sign of recognition. The room fell silent as time crept forward. A heavy air of mystery anchored them in place. Kelly glanced over at the puzzle on the shelf, then back to the book on the table.

Her head tilted to the side as her eyes narrowed. Her forehead bunched up as confusion took hold. She glimpsed between the puzzle and book once more, hoping an answer would magically appear overhead and explain what all this meant. Mere coincidence? Perhaps. But the creep factor of the items to occupy their time went up tenfold in less than ten minutes. The weight of their situation bore down on them as realization set back in.

"So... what do you think Skip and Billie are doing? They've been *checking out the rest of the house* for quite a while now." Jennifer laughed, attempting to lighten the mood.

Laughter echoed off the living room walls. Giggles ping-ponged down the hallway for the questionable couple to hear. The five women huddled closer together as each of them took turns spewing out ideas of what the missing two were up to. Life felt normal for a beat—like women gossiping around the proverbial water cooler.

"Well, I'm sure we have all figured out by now that Skip is a major hornball," Kelly admitted without hesitation.

"Uh, yeah. But Billie doesn't seem to realize it. Either that or she's willfully blind. Maybe it's the blonde hair. I hate to categorize people by appearance, but if the shoe fits..." Jennifer added.

"I don't know. Billie seems like a nice girl. Maybe she actually likes him," Nina tossed out in an effort to defend Billie in her absence.

"Who knows. She probably does like him. But him... what he said earlier... he seems to like anything with two legs and a vajayjay. No discrimination on his part whatsoever," Belinda stated, adding fuel to the fire.

Laughter erupted once more. Unrestrained chortles. Tears staining a few sets of cheeks. Kelly raised her hand, trying to speak between sharp inhalations. "Oh. My. God... that's too much. I can't. I can't take it."

The giggles died down—a few of them bent at the waist and clenching their sides—before Kristen jumped in. "Maybe we wait a little longer. Then, I say we can go check on them. Billie's a big girl. She willingly walked down the hall with a guy who was pretty open about being a nympho. Surely, he's used to finding different ways to get women to sleep with him. As long as I don't hear any screams, I'll ignore whatever they're up to."

"I'm good with him, as long as he doesn't attempt to hook up with me. Nowhere near my type," Jennifer said as the others nodded in agreement. "So... on to other topics."

Kristen held up the pad of paper and flipped it around

for everyone to see. "I've been working on meal planning for all of us. If that's okay?"

"Definitely okay. I'm no kitchen magician."

Kristen giggled at Belinda's response. "Lucky for everyone here, I kind of am. So, I took an inventory of everything in the cabinets. Granted, I can't make fancy meals from most of what's in there, but… I can make a lot of different things. So that definitely weighs in our favor."

"How many meals can we get out of what's in there? Roughly," Kelly asked.

"Well, I've figured out at least a week's worth of meals so far—breakfast, lunch, and dinner—and I haven't crossed everything off the inventory list yet. If everyone doesn't eat three meals a day, we'll obviously have more."

Jennifer raised her hand as if she needed permission to speak. The group stared at her and waited.

"I'm pretty easy to please. Usually eat once a day. Twice on occasion. Please, please, please" —Jennifer clasped her hands in prayer position in front of her mouth— "tell me there's coffee in the kitchen. You all won't like me much without my daily dose. All joking aside."

"I did find a bag of ground coffee in the cabinet. Some brand I've never heard of before, so I have no clue how it'll taste," Kristen reassured her.

"Hey, it's better than nothing. Seriously, me without coffee equals the rest of you being miserable. Like *lock that bitch away* kind of miserable."

A few of the women snickered. Jennifer simply shrugged at her honesty. When the sniggering simmered down, Belinda broached the topic which made them all scoot forward more.

"So, should we go check on them and make sure Billie is safe? Or make sure they haven't gotten *lost* in the bedroom? I mean, after all, Skip is the only *guy* in the group. Anyone else considered *he* is the psycho-killer? He said he was a locksmith. But was that some made-up bullshit to explain how he couldn't bust the locks?"

Nina, Jennifer, Kelly, and Kristen stared at Belinda slack-jawed and speechless. By their shared expressions, it was obvious none of them had considered the idea. That the person who brought them to the house could be Skip. He *was* the only male in a group.

Why would someone abduct six women and one man? It made no sense to them. If it were one man and one woman—a couple—it would be feasible. But this... there was no logical explanation. At least not right now.

Kelly was on her feet as her eyes darted to the hallway. She stared for a split-second before turning back to the group.

"I'm finding something to take with me—a weapon—and I'm heading down that hallway to check on them. You guys can either stay here or go with me. Don't care which you choose."

As she headed for the kitchen, the others rose from their seats and followed in her wake. When they sidled up to the kitchen, Kelly shuffled around, slamming drawers as she searched for her weapon of choice.

Kristen asked, "What are you looking for? Maybe I can help since I've already looked through the entire kitchen."

"Anything I can use. A butcher knife. A cleaver. Don't really care," Kelly stated harshly.

"Over here." Kristen opened a drawer at the far end near the stove. "This drawer is loaded with all kinds of gadgets. I'm sure you'll find what you're looking for in here."

Kelly riffled through the drawer and eventually withdrew a meat mallet. This mallet was larger and heavier than the original one they found. She twisted and turned it in her grasp, ogling the flat and spiked, tenderizer sides. Once satisfied with her selection, she told the others to arm themselves with their own weapon of choice.

Just to be on the safe side.

The others yanked open drawers and scavenged through the plethora of shiny kitchen implements. A minute later, the five women were armed like a kitchen army, ready to infiltrate and attack the enemy. Kelly wielded the mallet. Kristen armed with a solid wood rolling pin. Jennifer fisted the cleaver. Nina sported a heavy-gauge, steel roasting fork. And Belinda brandished a cast-iron skillet.

Armed and at the ready, the ladies tiptoed toward the hallway—only stopping when Kelly paused and held her hand in the air. She peered over her shoulder and tapped a finger to her ear. They acknowledged her covert gesture with a thumbs up.

Moving slower than a tortoise, Kelly tiptoed down the long hallway. She slowed further as they approached the first door—the bathroom. Peeking her head around the corner of the doorframe, she scanned the new bathroom interior before she flipped on the light.

No longer was the room this grungy, grimy filth-hole. Before, the walls and porcelain were stained brown and coated in mold. Now, the walls glowed bright white. A marble-topped black vanity with a deep sink and a large mirror overhead looked as if it was fresh from a showroom. Small stones served as a backsplash beneath and surrounding the mirror. All the fittings were a matte nickel finish and glimmered in the light emanating from the antique light fixture. The bathtub sparkled against the light —a pop of yellow glowing like the sun on the cloth shower curtain.

The entire appearance now modern and fresh and pristine. Light and cheery with a pop of color. The difference between the original version of the bathroom and the new and improved version were night and day.

The others caught a glimpse of the bathroom as Kristen audibly gasped. Kelly turned quickly, pressed a finger to her puckered lips, and shushed her. She waved between herself and the others, signaling them to back out slowly as she cut the light.

Stepping to the front of the pack once more, Kelly restarted their path to the next door. A few feet from the bathroom, she stopped in her tracks and stared at the photograph not there earlier in the day. She scrutinized it heavily as the group gathered around her, examining it alongside her.

As they each became aware of what the image was—a blindfolded woman strapped to a table and being tortured

—a hand slapped over each of their mouths. Although the house had flipped from some dilapidated shack into a beautiful home countless people dreamed of owning, it was littered with horrendous images. Presumably put up by the person who abducted them. Who knew what else they would come across as they ventured on.

Passing the photo on the wall, they crept into the first bedroom. No sign of Skip or Billie. They stopped and stared at the newly renovated first bedroom—with the exception of the weird doll collection—and did a quick, visual inventory of the room before exiting. Nothing in the room, at first glance, appeared out of the ordinary.

Moving down the hall, the triple-bolted door on the left came into view. Curiosity flooded Jennifer. She itched to try the handle. When she stepped up and twisted the lever, nothing happened. The door didn't budge. She shrugged, spun back around, and mouthed *I had to give it a try.*

A few feet farther, and on the opposite side of the hall, was the last bedroom. The door slightly ajar. Kelly crept up and peered inside. Her eye barely past the jamb, she scanned the room. Near a corner of the footboard, she spotted Skip and Billie.

Still fully clothed, Billie clutched Skip's biceps as he kissed his way up the side of her neck. Practically panting, she traced her hands down his arms and dropped them to his waist, gripping him more firmly. Skip cupped Billie's face with one hand while the other kneaded one of her petite breasts. He sucked and nibbled beneath her ear while Billie gasped at the ceiling.

Kelly stepped away from the gap, fisted her hands, and

rubbed her eyes as she tried to wipe away the visual forever etched into her brain. Kristen peered in the room next, backing away just as quickly. She stuck a finger in her mouth and pretended to gag. Jennifer, Belinda, and Nina briefly glanced at the spectacle before stepping back and silently laughing.

Kelly signaled for everyone to leave and head down the hall as she pulled the door shut. They tiptoed as if on a secret mission. When they broke free from the walls of the tight corridor, a quiet but audible laugh poured out of each of them. They pulled out a chair and sat at the dining table —each adding their own two cents about what they'd just witnessed.

The only thing the five women agreed upon... they wanted nothing to do with sex-junkie Skip.

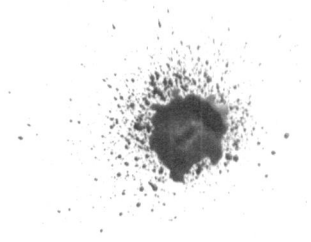

After a fit of giggles, the five women at the dining table clutched their stomachs. A few had tears streaming down their cheeks. This singular moment—sneaking a peek at Billie and Skip—bonded the five women outside the bedroom. They had a secret all their own to share and snigger about. The joke between them lowering their guard and lifting their spirits. The earlier fear of being trapped in this house slowly faded.

"I don't know about the rest of you, but I'm suddenly hungry," Jennifer announced. She glanced at the women nodding in agreement and clapped her hands.

"Cool. I can whip something up for everyone, if you're all okay with that?" Kristen asked.

Jennifer, Nina, Belinda, and Kelly stared at Kristen as if she were a saint. Stoic, they held her gaze a beat before saying *yes* in unison. Another fit of giggles ensued. The women in this house—minus one—fell into a comfortable routine, of sorts. Easy conversation. Endless laughter. Simple ease being near each other.

Kristen headed for the kitchen and chatted with the others through the open bar space between the kitchen and dining room. "Any requests? We don't have the whole kit and caboodle, but we do have variety. Sure I can improvise if need be."

Jennifer, Nina, Belinda, and Kelly regarded one another. A series of shrugs circulated around the table. No one expressed desire for anything specific.

"I think we've reached a unanimous decision of *we don't give a fuck*," Kelly said.

"Cool. I'll check out the list and pick one of the meals. Let you know how things are progressing in a bit."

Kristen consulted her notepad from earlier and figured out a meal most everyone would enjoy. Skimming her finger down the page, Kristen had a silent conversation with herself as she talked her way through making the meal. *Nope. Nope. Nope,* she thought as she trailed down the page. Then she stopped. Her finger hovered over the winner as a grin lit up her face. Decision made.

Immediately, Kristen buzzed around the kitchen. She lugged out one ingredient after another. Then she pulled out all the necessary tools—pots, pans, cutting board, utensils—and got to work.

Nina, Belinda, Jennifer, and Kelly lingered around the dining table, chitchatting and learning more about each other. Earlier, they shared snippets about themselves, but that was—more or less—to learn if any of them came from the same city or general area. As far as they could tell, none of them worked or lived near each other.

Nina was the first to divulge about her life. "Earlier, I told you all I'm a schoolteacher, but I didn't expand. Currently, I teach second graders at a private school. I've been working at the same school for fifteen years and love every moment of it. There's something special about teaching the younger children. They're like little sponges. Ready to absorb every bit of information you give them. Plus, they're eager to learn and grateful. It's beyond rewarding to pass knowledge on to another person, especially those who have years to grow into their wisdom. Also, it's wonderful to watch them flourish and become these amazing, unique individuals. They all learn the exact same lessons from me, but they interpret them differently. Watching them blossom always fascinates me."

Nina was introspective a moment as she relished over the simple life she led. She gathered her thoughts then continued. "I have a daughter, Michelle, who I just visited. Was heading home from her house when all this happened.

She lives in northern Georgia. Will probably be a week or more before she realizes I never called to say I arrived home safely. She leads a busy life with her husband. They're both realtors and own a business together. Hopefully everything will be back to normal before she realizes I haven't called." Nina hung her head low on her shoulders as she mumbled her last words.

Belinda, Kelly, and Jennifer sat silently and waited for Nina to continue. When Nina didn't utter another word, they took it as a sign she'd said all she planned to.

Jennifer stared at her with sad eyes, wanting to break up the sudden melancholy in the room.

"As I told everyone earlier, I work in a lab which experiments and discovers new, alternative ways to make faux leather. Something more cost-effective for consumers and also keeps the vegan community satisfied," Jennifer stated with pride in her voice.

"Thought there was already something out on the market as an alternative. Pleather, right? Isn't that, like, plastic leather?" Kelly asked with true curiosity.

"Plastic leather is an option on the market. But, with so many people becoming environmentally conscious nowadays, plastic is slowly fading. The world went from no plastic decades ago to an overabundance. Plastic is everywhere. Packaging, clothing—for added stretch, and even food. Companies, like the one I work for, have discovered so many different ways to create a leatherlike product by simply using plants. In the lab, we spend a lot of time figuring out which plants work better and how to process them to get the end result we're looking for."

Her job and the company which manufactured fake leather from plants mesmerized everyone. They took turns asking her a variety of questions—some she could answer, some she was unable to. But everyone seemed extremely fascinated by the woman who was a vegan leather lab technician.

"You guys are making my job sound like this super glamorous thing. It's really not. Most of the time, I'm cooking fruits and vegetables and foliage in ovens. Watching them to make sure they don't dry out too quickly or catch fire. Really, it's not that spectacular."

"Oh, alright. Well it's a hell of a lot more glamorous than being a manager at a convenience store alongside the highway. All I see, most of the time, is truckers or strange looking folks passing through town. Every once in a while, we get some real weirdos. People strolling around the store like it's Disney World, oohing and awing over snacks or pop. Or we get the folks who don't understand the concept of clothing. Others we had to stalk like the freaking police or something, watching to see if they shoplift. Frickin' punks. Such a pain in my ass."

"Yeah, but that's probably an easier job than mine," Jennifer proposed to Belinda.

"It's not that it's difficult. That's not what I meant. More like… there's nothing fulfilling about it. I get up every day, put on one of seven matching polos, slide into a black pair of pants, and wear the same nonslip, black work sneakers. There's no variety in my life. The only excitement I get is calling the cops on someone trying to steal something or buy cigarettes and/or alcohol under the legal age. It's repetitive and gets old pretty quick."

"I see what you mean," Kelly chimed in. "Is there anything you ever wanted to do?"

"God… it's been so long since I've thought about *me*. Not sure. I always liked painting. But there's no money in art, not unless you're some modern-day *Picasso*."

"Sadly true. Many people get discovered, though. It's just not something you hear about on the ten o'clock news."

"I suppose so. What about you, Kelly?"

Kelly fidgeted in her chair as she glanced around the table. "Like I said earlier, I'm a tattoo artist." She waved her hand up and down one arm, then the other, as if revealing ink sleeves on her skin like a game show host. "I love how my work allows me to be creative and have a little bit of freedom. One thing I'm losing my mind over right now is not having had a cigarette in… *Fuck!* I don't know what time it is. Or what day. It's been way too fucking long. Not that I've checked, but I haven't found any anywhere. Plus, I'm sure no one wants me smoking around them."

"I've been there before," Jennifer responded. "Smoked for years, but finally gave it up almost two years ago. Wasn't easy. You just have to find other things to distract you. Maybe we can see if there're any toothpicks in the kitchen. Sometimes, just having something in your mouth, like a toothpick, helps with the physical habit."

"Yeah, think I'll go rummage through the cabinets and drawers again. Maybe ask Kristen if she's seen any. Thanks, man."

"Sure thing."

The women peeked over at Kristen. Her hands were layered in white as she rolled dough on the counter. Completely absorbed with her task, Kristen hadn't noticed how the chatter ceased and all eyes were now on her.

Kelly scooted her chair back and walked over to the counter, watching Kristen run the rolling pin in one direction, and then the opposite. "What are you making?"

Kristen's head popped up as she learned she had gained an audience. Her cheeks pinked, but she continued rolling. "Chicken and dumplings. The chicken won't be fresh, but canned is better than nothing at all. I'm making the dough for the dumplings first. Then I'll get started on the rest."

"That sounds fantastic. Hey, do you remember seeing any toothpicks while you were doing inventory?"

"Uh, yeah. Think so." She pointed at a drawer to her right, near the kitchen entrance. "I think they're in the top second drawer."

Kelly stepped around the counter and opened the drawer. Inside, she located a box of toothpicks alongside some bamboo skewers and other miscellaneous kitchen knickknacks. Snagging the box from the drawer, she popped a toothpick between her lips and sighed. The oral fixation relieved almost immediately.

She twiddled the small, wooden stick side to side between her lips, shifting it every few seconds. "It may not satiate my need for nicotine, but it'll help for the time being. Thanks."

Kristen nodded as her eyes focused on the lightly herbed dough spread out on the counter. When the dough thickness was to her liking, she set the rolling pin down, and fetched a knife. She cut the flattened dough into small squares. By the time she'd finished cutting all the dough, there was enough for each person to have a dozen to themselves.

The four women leaned against the kitchen counter—on the bar facing the dining area—completely fascinated as they watched Kristen work. Cooking wasn't foreign to any of these women. Was just a fact they usually cooked more simplistically. No point in making lots of food when you were the only person eating.

Nina pointed to the vegetables on the far counter. "Do you need help with cutting those?"

"Sure. If you'd like, you can dice up the onion. Unless the burning eyes part bothers you."

"No, I'm good. Would love to help. It's been a while since I've really cooked for more than anyone besides myself. Not so easy to make dishes like this for one, unless you're prepared to eat it for days or freeze several containers of it."

"I think we all understand that a little too much," Belinda said. "Think that might be part of the reason we were all *chosen*. Because we have no one at home."

Silence fell over the group. Kristen and Nina paused their vegetable dicing. Nina peered up from the onion and scanned their faces. "I think that makes us all sound sad and pathetic. Living alone is my choice. If I wanted, I could find a roommate. But I choose my lifestyle. So, I refuse to be sad about it."

Eerie silence fell over the room again. Each woman was deep in her own thoughts. Wondering if their outcome would've been different if they had someone to come home to. None of them would learn the answer, though. Because how could they? It's not as if the mystery man who'd brought them to this house planned to magically appear and tell them yes or no. Only time would tell.

Nina began cutting the onion into slices, then chopping the slices into smaller pieces. For someone who wasn't professionally trained to work in a kitchen, Nina was pleased with her work as she stepped back to observe the tiny onion squares on her cutting board.

Kristen meticulously cut the carrots and celery into small cubes. Once cut to the appropriate size, she grabbed the twenty-four-quart stockpot and set it on the stovetop. The pot was created for an industrial kitchen and could easily hold enough soup for fifty people. There would definitely be leftovers.

Opening the fridge, Kristen took out a stick of butter. She cut off a large chunk and tossed it into the pot. Once melted, she scraped the carrots into the pot, explaining to everyone watching how the denser root vegetables took longer to cook. When she was pleased with how much they'd softened, she added the celery and had Nina add the onion.

They cooked in the pot until the onion started becoming translucent. Then Kristen added more butter. *More butter always makes everyone happy*, Kristen thought. Once melted, she scooted the vegetables to the outside of the pot and added a small amount of flour to the butter. She told everyone she was making a roux—a base which made the soup thick and creamy.

Completely mesmerized by the process, they all simply nodded. Each of them glad Kristen knew what she was talking about. After stirring the roux for a minute or two, Kristen added a splash of milk, a handful of dried herbs, and several cans of vegetable broth. She stirred it a little longer before adding water to the mix, followed by a few cans of the chicken.

"Now we just need to let that simmer on the stove for twenty to thirty minutes and then we can add the dumplings."

With everything thrown into the oversized pot, the women stood silent and stared at each other, and wondered what to do next. Kristen mentioned cleaning up the kitchen. In the blink of an eye, the others offered to lend a hand. When they finished, they all settled in the living room and waited for the timer to go off.

More gossip ensued regarding the happenings in one particular bedroom at the end of the hall.

Unbeknownst to them, it would be the craziest and most memorable sex anyone experienced. Little did they know, the group would never be the same when the moment came to an end. For now, the five women sitting in the living room were happily discussing how crazy the whole scenario was. Right now, everything was as normal as it could be in their circumstances.

Right now, all seven of them were still alive.

CHAPTER FIVE

SKIP

GOD, her skin tastes fucking delicious. Like honey and vanilla. If she'd let me, I'd rip her clothes off right now and fuck her a hundred times over. But Billie doesn't seem like the type of woman I should ravage that way. No telling how long we'll be trapped in this twisted situation. I have to keep her in my good graces.

I have to keep her pleading for more.

If taking my time is what I have to do, then that is what has to happen. I need an all-access pass to this woman. The one woman in this house who doesn't see through my bull-shit. The one woman that wilts at my facade. I need her like an alcoholic needs three fingers of scotch.

I lick my way up the side of her neck, sucking on her earlobe a moment before biting it tenderly. When I draw back, her willowy frame relaxes in my hands and her limbs loosen and become more carefree. One hand roams my backside, skimming the waistline of my pants. Heat spreads like wildfire across my skin as she scrapes her nails along my flesh.

I cup her face in my palms and lure her closer to me

before slamming my mouth on hers with ravenous hunger. A hunger eager to devour every inch of her body. An aching desire to find out if she tastes just as delicious at the apex of her thighs. It takes every ounce of restraint to dial down the ache in my groin. To let her guide me and feel in control.

Thankfully, she's driving us in a direction which benefits us both. Billie's body responds like no other woman I have previously been with. Her tongue jets out and tangles with mine. Her hips grind against me. No doubt, she feels the thick length of my cock through my jeans.

I continue rubbing against her wanton body and bask in her expressions as sensation consumes her. Goads her. Has a moan slipping from her lips. The tempo of our kiss is frenzied. Eager hands skirt up and down my back. Nails dig in and forge a path down to my ass before she grabs hold.

This teenage foreplay is monotonous. Same shit, new body. Don't get me wrong, foreplay has its place. But this is child's play.

And I need more. More than hungry lips and heavy breaths. What I need is bare, heated flesh. Wet lips—both sets. Plump breasts and taut nipples. Begs and screams of *yes* and *more* and *ohmyfuckinggod*.

Breaking our kiss, I silently beg to fuck her. The ache to strip her bare and throw her on the bed sits heavy in my scrotum. Doe eyes stare back at me with a hint of confusion. I slip my hands under the edge of her cotton shirt and all her confusion vanishes. As I skim my fingertips along the skin under her navel, a tremor ripples through her from head to toe.

Before she learns my next move, I yank her shirt up—forcing her arms to the ceiling—jerk it off her body and toss it to the floor. I reach for the button on her skin-tight pants and release it from its confining hole with deft fingers. Her mouth forms a small *O* as she sucks in a sharp breath.

Exhilaration streams from her every pore, flowing off her in waves. Without a doubt, she is as desperate as I am. Tugging down her zipper, I expose the thin elastic band of her black panties. I stroke my fingertip back and forth along the top edge of the soft material, smiling when another round of shivers ripples through her body.

Slipping my finger below the material, her soft curls brush against my skin as I comb my fingers through them. The hunger inside me kicks up another notch.

Fuck!

I need to consume her pussy. *Now.* My hands go to both sides of her waist, fist her pants, and wrench them down. Foreplay time is most definitely over.

Her pants bunch at her ankles. She shifts her arms front and center with her hands clasped to hide her panties. Taking hold of one of her forearms, I slowly unlock her hands and step closer to her. "Don't hide from me. Soon enough, I'll be inside you. After, you'll never want to wear clothes near me again."

She locks eyes with me for a moment and scrutinizes my words. After she finds what she's looking for, she caves and drops her arms to her sides. Taking a few steps back, I scan the lines and curves of her scantily covered body. A greedy smile highlights my face when I notice her bra and panties match—not just the same color, but a matching set. Both garments have straps with the same lacey pattern, the same sheen, and the same patches of sheer material in the best places.

How many women wear lingerie sets on a daily basis? Not many I know. Hell, some of my dates wore cotton panties with childish patterns and bras which needed replacing.

But Billie... Billie is a little fucking sex kitten. No woman purchases lingerie sets without hoping someone will see them. Some say they purchase them as a confidence booster, but I think they're full of shit. I wonder how many matching bra and panty sets Billie has?

I step closer to her again. My dick aches and is hard as marble. My balls so tight and swollen they scream for relief. I slide my hands under her arms and lift her off the floor, tossing her on the bed and tugging the pants from her ankles.

She lies on the bed, props herself up on her elbows, and watches me as I undress. In no time, my shirt and pants join hers on the floor. Kneeling on the mattress, I crawl my way up and hover above her. Her chest rises and falls rapidly. Her breath hot under my lips. Lowering myself, I press my hips to hers and grind my erection against her cleft.

I wasn't sure what to expect, but was shocked when her chest arched off the bed. When her breasts smashed against my chest and begged for more. With a roll of my hips, I drive forward again. And again. And again. Her jaw goes slack and a moan rips from her throat.

Fuck me sideways.

This woman made my balls blue in three-point-five

seconds. As sexy as her lingerie is, the bra needs to go. I need to roll her bare nipples with my fingers. The panties also need to vanish. I need my cock in her sweet hole now.

My hand slinks around to her back and fumbles with the clasp of her bra. Once unhooked, her breasts fall free from the cups. I slide the straps off her arms and toss it to the side. Sweeping kisses down her sternum, I pause as I hover between her pert tits.

Her breasts are perfect. Absolute, one hundred percent perfection. Two small, plump works of beauty. Their peaks taut and begging for my touch.

I wrap my lips around her left, sucking the soft tissue into my mouth and biting her nipple before switching to the right and repeating the process.

Rising to sit on my haunches, I skim a finger down her midline. When I reach the elastic edge of her panties, I grasp the material and jerk up, exposing her curls and causing the material to wedge in the folds of her pussy.

A hiss resonates from her lips. Her hands swipe at mine, fighting against my clutch on the dainty material. I shake my head.

"Tsk, tsk, tsk. Won't be like this for long. Remember Billie, sometimes you can find pleasure in the pain. Think of the pressure on your clit. Focus on that."

Grazing my fingertips along the curve of her inner thigh, I tease the bikini line of her curls. Inching closer to my goal, I drag the panties down her legs and toss them aside. My eyes lock on her apex and zero in on her glistening folds. My tongue darts out and I lick my bottom lip.

Fuck. Cannot wait to taste her.

My fingers trace the trimmed patch of hair above her clit. I tease her just enough to boost her insatiable appetite up a notch. The desire for more screams in my head—both of them—but I desperately want her to show how badly she wants me. As if she hears my thoughts, she bucks her hips off the bed and presses her pussy against my palm.

My gaze locks with hers and I remain motionless, teasing and driving her wild. I torture her over and over again. Dragging out the inevitable. Minutes later, we're still in the same position. Eyes wide. Hips pressed to mine. She repeats the motion three more times, silently pleading with me to do something other than tease her.

I plan to take this further, but I want her to crave it so badly she would be willing and able to take it repetitively.

And then she changes the game.

When she realizes I have no intention of caving to her will, she switches tactics. Like a voyeur unable to look away, I watch as she rolls two fingers around her nipple. She grinds against me and moans in pleasure. After grinding against me enough to rub her juices along my shaft, she shifts to the other breast and repeats the process.

When she finishes that line of torture, she glides down her belly to her waist.

Are my eyes deceiving me? She is definitely upping the ante. Lost in the sight of her, a second passes before it dawns on me her hand is between her legs. Circling her clit. Moaning without care.

Fucking hell. Consider me a dead man.

She is unmanning me. Right here. Right now.

Reluctantly, I lift her fingers away and drag them over

my tongue, sucking the sweet nectar from her digits. Without further preamble, I slip a finger inside her. Slick, warm walls clamp down on me. The ache to shove my cock inside her grows more unbearable by the second. I withdraw my finger to the distal knuckle, then thrust forward again. I relish at the view of her. Jaw slack. Breath ragged.

She is undeniably hot and one hundred percent ready for me to fuck her. I toy with her more. Kick her arousal into overdrive. Before fucking her, I yearn to see her orgasm bloom on her skin at least once. Pumping my finger in and out of her, my cock swells as she pants heavily and her body climbs higher. Small, high-pitched moans fill the room.

Harder. Faster. My fingers pump in and out of her, curling at the distal joint. I stare between her legs then gaze up her body to her face. Her breathing intensifies as her cries bleed into one another.

And then the magic happens.

Her walls tighten and clench my fingers, milking me as if I were the only source able to quench her thirst. Her face pinks. Every lick of skin I see glows with a light sheen.

When her body settles, I withdraw my fingers and bring them to my tongue. Trapping them in my mouth, I close my eyes and taste the heavenly flavor of her pussy. Salty and sweet and a hint of tang. The taste of her is sensory overload and drives my libido to new heights.

A sudden realization hits and halts me in my tracks.

Goddamn son of a bitch! This cannot be happening right now.

Billie furrows her brows and stares at me, confused. "What's wrong?"

"I don't have a *motherfucking* condom. I don't fuck without them. No matter what," I tell her. This would be my goddamn misfortune. Some sick motherfucker locks me in a house full of women and I can't fuck a goddamn one of them. Real piece of shit.

We look everywhere except at each other. Billie points to the small table beside the bed. "That has a drawer. Check it. Maybe you'll get lucky. Twice," she says, hopeful. A smile lights up her face as she waggles her brows.

It's worth a shot. Seriously, what do I have to lose? Right about now, I'd take any substitutions. *Hell*, if I find nothing in here, I'll walk out to the kitchen—butt-ass naked—and grab some plastic wrap. I don't give a fuck. My dick is getting wrapped and fucked. No matter what.

I open the drawer and am surprised to see it's full of random stuff—pen, paper, a cassette Walkman, and a bunch of other miscellaneous stuff. I shuffle the items around in the drawer as Billie watches me. I shift a couple things to the side and the gods rain down on me. Because there it is. In all its glory.

The answer to my prayers. The one thing I desperately need.

Whoever our captor is, they obviously understand I'm a man with unrelenting needs. Secretly, I praise them and pray there are more condoms where this one came from.

I tear open the foil package, pinch the head and roll the condom down my shaft. Billie lays back against the bed, spreads her legs farther apart, and teases her slick pink pussy. I crawl back onto the bed, position myself above her and line my cock against her slit, ready to ram into her.

She clutches my biceps and squeezes them tight enough I feel the bite of her nails. The sensation jacks me up to Mach ten as I slam forward and thrust my cock inside her.

Fuck! Fuck! Fuck!

I don't move an inch while I give myself a minute to bask in the glory of her hot pussy wrapped around my dick. But also giving her a minute to acclimate to my size. She is so *fucking tight.*

Damn, she feels so fucking good. It has been far too long since I've felt a cunt this tight.

Her eyes pop open—pupils fully dilated and eyes glossy. Without a word, I know she is ready. That she wants more. Needs it.

I rock my hips back, leaving only the tip inside her, and then slam forward again. Her nails pierce my skin and I hiss at the mixture of pain and pleasure. The sensation drives me wild and I ramp up my rhythm. I rock back, then drive forward—a loud moan belts from her lips. It's a direct line to my throbbing dick.

I pump in and out of her—faster, harder. Her body scoots up the bed with each thrust. I slide a hand under her neck and hold her in place while I pound her.

God, she feels so fucking good.

Her chest heaves, rising and falling faster than a marathon. Her breath heavy as it heats the skin on my neck. Her moans echo in my ear and unleash a beast inside me. I pick up the pace with each new sound she makes. The harder I fuck her, the louder her pitch grows.

And she's close.

I feel it.

On the cusp of detonation.

Her walls constrict around my cock as I piston my cock in and out of her as rapidly as possible. Tremors ripple throughout her body, starting with her limbs and conjoining at her core. A guttural noise rips from her throat as a smattering of red splotches paint her face and chest. Watching her orgasm is a phenomenal sight to behold. Intensity and passion take center stage and it is a beautiful thing to witness.

Once her body calms, I pick up the pace, seeking my own orgasm. The onset is seconds away, and I yearn to feel the relief that follows. A deep pressure wells up inside me. Heat and electricity surge like wildfire to my dick. My balls contract. There. Right on the brink of the most amazing bliss.

Bam!

An explosion fires inside of me, igniting like a stick of dynamite. Cum shoots out of me at high velocity, my seed filling the latex sheath. My body is drenched with sweat. I hover above her with ragged breaths tearing from my lungs and my heart jackhammering in my chest.

Holy fuck!

I want to fuck her again, but I need a minute.

A minute to catch my breath. A minute so I can get my dick back up. If I asked her, no doubt she'd want to go another round. She has been eager and open about wanting to fuck all along.

Just as I'm about to voice my idea—about to withdraw and remove the condom—something stops me. Something is off. Something doesn't feel right. Matter-of-fact, something feels the complete opposite of right.

A burning sensation trickles across my cock and spreads to my balls as both slowly start to numb. But the sensation —or lack thereof—doesn't stop there, though. The tops of my thighs and the meaty mass of my glutes tingling. Every muscle beneath my skin numbs one centimeter at a time. Within seconds, I lose feeling from my upper mid-thigh to the base of my abdomen.

What the hell is happening to me?

Billie's face scrunches in worry as she watches my expression change with every passing second. "Are you okay?"

I want to tell her I'm fine. Not to worry about anything. But I can't manage to say the words. Something is definitely wrong and I don't know how to explain what is happening. *Hell*, I don't even know what the fuck is happening to me. Whatever it is, it cannot be good.

"Uh, yeah, sorry. I think, maybe, I'm having some sort of allergic reaction or something to the condom. Are you okay?"

"Yeah, fine. Great, actually."

Well I'm glad *she's* feeling spectacular. At least one of us is basking in positive results. The loss of sensation spreads farther along my body. My leg now numb to my knee, and my torso numb to the base of my sternum.

Panic sets in. My heart pounds like tightly clenched fists against my ribcage. My lungs heave, desperate for more oxygen. Attempting to move my hips, I manage to withdraw from Billie. I waste every ounce of effort I possess as my body slowly sinks rather than rises.

"What do you mean you think you're having some allergic reaction to the condom? Has that ever happened to you before?" Billie asks, anxiety lacing her tone.

"Never. Maybe these are made from some kind of weird material or there was something on the inside. I don't know."

"What can I do? How can I help you?"

If I knew the magic answer, I would have done it already. That's what I want to tell her. But instead, I say, "I really don't fucking know. I can't feel half my body right now and it's freaking me the *fuck* out."

My legs are almost fully numb as they buckle under my weight. I shift slightly and drop onto Billie. Bracing my arms on either side of her, I hope I can support myself above her.

My torso is on the precipice of complete numbness. The thump of my heartbeat fades in my chest. I have no way of knowing, but I hope the organ doesn't fail. A new surge of panic courses through the parts of me I can still feel. I don't know what the fuck is going on and I have absolutely no idea how to fix it.

Is this what paralysis feels like when people experience it after an accident or traumatic event? *Holy shit.* This cannot be happening to me. I have fucked hundreds of women. Used so many condoms I should own stock in all the companies. This has got to be some kind of fluke. A joke meant to teach me a lesson for using women throughout most of my life.

Ha ha, you sick fucker. Joke's over. Cut this shit out. Right now!

The tops of my shoulders start to prickle as numbness sets in. My lungs are on fire. I take a deep breath, in the hopes the cool air in the room will quench the burning in my chest. Not even remotely close. If anything, the more I breathe, the stronger it burns.

The numbness spreads down my biceps and creeps its way along until it reaches my elbow. A pins and needles sensation spreads across my neck and lower jaw. Before I realize what's happening, my arms collapse beneath me and my body drops its full weight on top of Billie, pinning her to the mattress.

My body is motionless. My neck won't rotate and my face lands in her hair. I'm aware of the pressure of her body trying to shift me off of her, but I don't budge. Frozen in place, I'm unable to help her or myself. *Fuck! Why can't I move?*

For a moment, it sounds as if she is saying something—maybe shouting at the top of her lungs—but everything is muffled.

My breathing picks up and turns shallow. The whooshing sound of my pulse behind my ears is no longer audible.

I think I'm fucking dying. *What the hell else could this be?*

I'm not ready to die. I have barely lived.

The numbness spreads to my eyes and my vision morphs into this cloud of meaningless blobs and colors. Nothing makes sense anymore. I have lost almost every sensory perception I possess. An utterly hopeless sex fanatic.

The room steadily becomes darker—going from blindingly bright to complete and utter darkness in a matter of seconds.

This is it. This is the end. The end of my life.

But at least I did it my way. Doing the one thing that made me who I am. And I did it pretty damn well if I do say so myself.

At least I went out with an orgasmic bang with a pretty hot piece of ass. I cannot think of a better way to die. Death by orgasm. Worse things could have happened. If I could voice my final thoughts, I would tell Billie I'm the luckiest guy on the planet. I would thank her and wish her well.

But I can't. Because the dead don't speak.

CHAPTER SIX

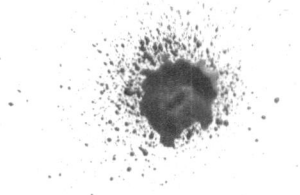

BILLIE

OH MY GOD! Oh my god! Oh my god!

What the hell is happening to him?

His body just collapsed on me. He is literally dead-weight from head to toe. I fidget relentlessly and manage to wiggle my arms underneath him. After way too much exertion, I press my palms flat to his chest. I take a minute to breathe—which is challenging as hell with a two-hundred-plus-pound man on top of you.

With all I can muster, I exert every ounce of strength in my arms to lift him off of me. I grit my teeth, tighten my core, and squeeze my eyes shut as I thrust my arms up. But no matter how much leverage I put behind my force, Skip doesn't budge. He lays over me like a body bag of bricks, slowly crushing me.

I scream for help in the hopes one of the others will hear me and come to our rescue. But with the gravity of Jupiter pressing down on me, my screams are easily muffled and squashed. Breathing is a challenge all its own, let alone yelling.

Short, quick gasps heat my ear. Not like earlier when he

moaned through his orgasm. There is no sensuality in this scenario.

His head lays on my hair and traps me, keeping me from rotating my head. Out of nowhere, claustrophobia hits me and I jerk my head left and right and up, working to yank my hair out from under him. With each jerk, a sting pierces my scalp and my eyes water. But I accept the pain. Each forceful movement of my head loosens my hair from its trap.

Then his breathing stops.

"Skip? Skip, are you okay?" I ask, worried.

I count to thirty and he still hasn't responded.

"Skip! Skip, can you hear me?" I shriek.

Still nothing.

No words. No sounds. Not a single movement.

Absolutely nothing.

His weight has me completely pinned in place. My chest constricts and compresses under the pressure. I don't care how it happens, or what miracle needs to be performed, but I need him off of me. Now. No way I'll be able to lay trapped under him for much longer.

One last time, I scream for his attention. And once again, there is no response from him.

Not exactly sure what has happened to him—if he had a heart attack or a stroke or some strange reaction, as he suggested. What I do know... I no longer hear or feel him breathing. His full body weight is bearing down on every inch of me. And something horrible has happened to him.

Is he dead? A chill slithers up my spine.

I wiggle to change the position of my arms and place

them in a more feasible position to lift him. With my arms bent at the elbows and hands gripping his shoulders, I take a deep breath, dig deep, and shove up with brutal force on the exhale.

His body rises a couple inches above mine and I shift him to the side a few inches before he topples back on top of me. With the minor shift, my breathing is much closer to normal. I take a few deep breaths and relish in the relief it brings. Then I make the next attempt to lift him. One hand remains trapped beneath him against his chest, while my other hand is free and clutching on to the opposite shoulder.

Counting to three, I inhale deeply and lift up. His weight shifts again. The minor alteration allows me to slide out from under him and roll away.

Gasping, my lungs burn as they suck in the missed oxygen. The farther I roll away from Skip's lifeless body, the more I notice. His eyes remain wide open—pupils fully dilated as they gaze into the distance at nothingness. His lips are slightly parted—a blue tinge replacing the normal pink hue.

I stare at him and wonder what the hell happened. I hug myself as a shiver of fear prickles my bare flesh. A horrid feeling twists in my gut and makes me nauseous. Not quite sure what causes it, but whatever it is, it cannot be good.

When I regain my focus, I stare at Skip's open mouth. The way his tongue dangles lazily between his lips. I nudge his foot. The extremity jostles with ease, but elicits no response from him.

Skip really is dead.

Did *I* kill him?

Was the sex too much for him? An idiotic thought, but that's where my mind travels.

Who dies from having sex? Old people. And let's face it, Skip is—was—no spring chicken.

This man stood in the other room and told all of us that he was some sort of sex freak. How truthful was that statement? Considering he just died while having sex? He is—was—a little overweight. His weight couldn't be the determining factor. One of the last things he told me was how he couldn't feel his body. Thought he was having some sort of allergic reaction to the condom. Or the condom was tampered with.

Shit.

What if whatever killed him spread to me?

Does this mean *I'm* going to die too? *Oh my god!*

I rub my hands up and down my biceps—occasionally squeezing and pinching and checking to see if I can still feel my own touch. A rush of gratitude flows through me when I recognize my own touch. I continue examining the rest of my body and smile when I discover everything appears to be normal.

Thank you, thank you, thank you. If there's a god in this life, I thank you.

Taking one last look at Skip, I step away from his body. I want to leave this room—leave this place—and never look back. But my gut instinct tells me it will never happen.

I walk across the room where my underwear lay on the floor. Bending over, I pick them up and slip them on.

As I slide the straps of my bra to my shoulders, a gurgle

echoes in the room behind me. I latch the bra hooks and slowly spin around. My stomach clenches as the bubbling rings out again.

I inch my way back toward the bed and stop at the footboard. A second later, a garbled gasp from Skip greets me.

Running to his side, I shake his shoulders and yell his name. His vacant, black eyes stare back at me while his tongue hangs lifeless between his lips. I shake him again and the gurgling dislodges from his throat—louder—as his face remains stone cold.

Holy shit.

Is this what I think it is? I have only heard about stuff like this. But who actually witnesses this kind of shit? No one I have ever known.

His body does it one last time. Grunting and frothing as if something is lodged in his airway, trying to escape.

Death rattle.

Is that what they call it? When your body has given up fighting. When your body no longer fights to save your life. When you are officially dead.

Has he been lying there, semi-lucid, for the last however many minutes? Mentally fighting to live while his body slowly gave up. *Oh, god.*

Could I have helped him? Given him CPR? Ran out of the room and screamed for help? Guilt washes over me as the reality of him being alive sets in. Was there really anything I could have done? Or was it too late? Two questions bound to haunt me for the rest of my life.

I drop to the floor and crawl as far away from Skip as humanly possible. The large room slowly closes in on me as

I inch across the floor. Reaching one of the corners, I press my back against the wall and draw up my knees, hugging them tight to my chest. I rock back and forth and allow the motion to soothe me.

Resting the side of my face on my knees, I continue rocking in place as I consider all I could have done to fix this situation. How it could have ended differently. I question every choice made since I woke up in this foreign place.

Why did this happen to me? What have I done to deserve this?

Truly, I'm not a bad person. Sure, I have made bad decisions, but not intentionally. And never to hurt anyone. So why did this person—whoever captured us—choose me? What qualities make me so special to a psychopath?

Was I too outgoing? Too noticeable? Too desperate for attention?

Perhaps the answer to the last three questions is yes, yes, and yes.

I did enjoy when men doted on me. When they fawned over me and treated me with gifts. If I sit down and think honestly about this, the undivided attention is the main reason I love the karaoke stage. Belting out lyrics and shaking my hips. So men ogle me. If I was lucky, I got a free drink or two every night I sang. Those drinks helped diminish my loneliness.

Perhaps this is retribution. Payback for every man I rejected after they gave me what I wanted. Punishment for every hookup I denied last minute. Penalty for the men I hooked up with and abandoned once they passed out.

Vengeance for the men I hooked up with and stole money from before I fled.

I suppose I'm not as good a person as I originally thought. Perhaps this is my own personal hell. Maybe none of this is real. Perhaps it's all a figment of my imagination and my soul is in shackles being tortured in a chamber far beneath Earth's mantle.

Until today, I never batted an eye at karma. Now… karma is giving me a dose of my own medicine. Payback for every single, solitary horrible deed I have committed in my lifetime. Payment for all the careless crimes I have swept under the rug. My just desserts sit on a silver platter as this psycho slowly spoon feeds them to me.

I hug my legs tighter as my body sways forward then back. As I stare at Skip's lifeless body on the bed, I wonder if he would still be alive if I weren't so desperate for attention. More than likely, the answer would be a resounding yes. No one else in the house seems to care much for him. If I would have kept to myself—maybe been a little colder toward him—perhaps he wouldn't currently be lying on the bed, cold and lifeless.

Releasing one of my hands, body still rocking in place, I smack my temple. The initial *thwack* creates a sharp pain above my ear. "You deserve the pain," I tell myself. After what I did, I deserve so much more. I strike myself again, harder this time. I bunch my fingers into a fist and do it again. And again. And again.

I drop my hand and my knuckles thump against the wood. Glancing up at Skip—my temple throbbing—I apologize to him. Tell him how sorry I am this happened to him.

That I'm sorry he was trapped in this house with me. How I was too eager for attention. And I wasn't strong enough to say no. How horrible I am because I couldn't do anything to save his life. But most of all…

How sorry I am for being responsible for his death.

If it had been any other woman, no doubt he would still be alive.

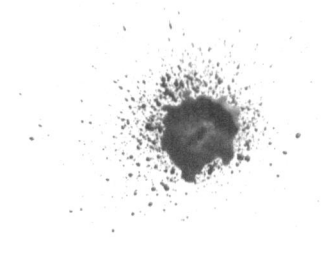

CAPTOR

Any minute now.

Any minute and the first of them will fall victim to my game.

My eyes are glued to the screen. A heaping bowl of buttery popcorn and my favorite bottle of pale ale sits on the small table beside me. Digging my hand into the butter-licious snack, I grab a handful of popped kernels and toss them in my mouth. Then wash the delicious salty taste down with a swig of ale before repeating the process.

After watching these people for the last six months, I have figured out several of their habits and tells. Honestly, learning these tidbits about my victims is essential. Makes the capture so much easier. As well as the retention. I gain an understanding of what each of them likes. What each of them dislikes. What turns them on. What makes them sick to their stomach. As well as what they love to eat.

Initially, they all want to leave. No matter their individual temperament, no matter how strong or weak they are, they each experience the same anxiety in the first hours. But then I switch things up. Change the scenery. And soon they settle. Soon they become comfortable in their camaraderie. Through conversation, they eventually learn their common denominator...

How utterly alone each and every one of them is.

Some of them alone by choice. Others alone for miscellaneous reasons. As I got to know each one of them—learning their personalities and quirks and habits—I discovered they would be my next, best experiment. I curated only the best of the best. The ones who would fulfill the void between my lungs, if only for a blink.

Several years have passed since one of my experiments included a man. Men can be irrational and unpredictable. Not many of them show their cards. Most have a consistent poker face. But when I stumbled across Skip, I instantly knew he was the real deal. He flaunted his tail feathers proudly and I couldn't resist adding him to the game. Honestly, he made it too easy.

I had been watching a woman for ten days. She was young and attractive and far too easy to lure in. She had been on several dates in the ten days I watched her. Each guy she dated was through an online dating website. On the tenth day, she went on a date with Skip.

I sat two tables away from them and eavesdropped as they discussed random foolishness. There was flirting from both parties—him more so than her. The more I listened to his constant sexual innuendos, the more fascinated I became. After twenty minutes, I discovered my attraction had switched gears. I was no longer interested in the curly-haired brunette I'd invested a week and a half following. Instead, I had become completely obsessed with Skip.

He was open and honest with each of the women he dated. He spoke nothing but truth when he told them he wasn't looking for long-term commitment. All he wanted was sex. Plain and simple. He would go through the rigma-role of the date—small talk and jokes and laughter, sharing a meal, him picking up the tab—as long as, when the date ended, they had sex. He disclosed his every desire to each woman, not fazed if she wasn't on board. There was always another woman around the corner.

He was exactly what I wanted in my collection.

My beautiful, priceless collection.

Shaking away the recent memory, I watch two of the live feeds on the screen. One feed comes from a camera hidden in the crown molding above the bedroom door. The other feed streams from a camera hidden in an artificial plant resting on the top of the dresser, the angle almost the complete opposite.

I munch on popcorn as Skip gets Billie off with his fingers. His erection indicates how eager he is to make her reach climax again. He rises from the bed and his expression becomes forlorn. I know exactly what he has just realized, but I hope he is smart enough to think past it.

As if I can predict the future, I hear him mumble on about not having a condom and refusing to have unprotected sex. This was one little fact I learned in the beginning with Skip. No condom equals no sex. Period. No matter how desperate he was, no matter how swollen his cock and balls were, he wasn't willing to take that sort of risk.

Billie suggests he look inside the drawer of the nightstand. Exactly what I was hoping would happen. Skip riffles through the drawer, shoving the uppermost contents to the side. In a eureka moment, he pulls out the square package and holds it in the air as if it's an Olympic gold medal.

I watch with keen anticipation as he tears open the condom wrapper and slides the latex into place. It fascinates me. How he was unable to decipher the packaging and how it is a bit different than a normal condom wrapper. Or maybe he just doesn't give a damn. Maybe he was so desperate for sex that he paid no attention.

I spent days creating that wrapper. I tore off a sheet of wax paper and cut it a little bigger than a normal condom wrapper package. Then I'd decorated the outside of it with fake branding—calling it some *natural* condom—thinking that would help make the package seem more believable. Then I'd found a small crimping tool, and heated the metal and sealed two of the sides first. After opening up the real condom wrapper, I carefully unrolled the condom and coated the inside with a thin layer of succinylcholine. With gloved hands, I carefully rolled the condom back up and placed it in the new packaging I created—sealing the last two edges with the heated crimper.

Succinylcholine isn't something too many people are familiar with. Majority of the time, it's a paralytic injected into the recipient. The way I coated the inside of the condom when Skip ejaculates, he should receive a minute dose. Enough to do the deed. By itself, the chemical isn't a killer. It all boils down to what it does to your body.

Skip continues his relentless endeavor with Billie, her body reaching its tipping point for second time. As her breathing calms and her sounds begin to fade, Skip drives himself forward. I know his only thought right now is achieving climax. He lives and breathes to orgasm.

And honestly, I am just as eager for him to get there, too.

He thrusts forward two more times and then it happens. I read it in his body language. In the contortions of his expression. I have watched this exact moment occur time and time again. He was victorious. And now, I will be too.

Skip slows the pace of his hips, then finally stops altogether. His face lights up with pure elation and the hungry desire for more. He opens his mouth and says something, pauses, then snaps it shut. His brows pinch together as he cocks his head to the side.

It's happening. It's fucking happening.

This is the first time I have introduced succinylcholine into one of my experiments. All the research says it doesn't take too long before the person experiences full paralysis. Maybe a minute or two. But that's using the conventional form of injection. I am excited to witness the results from my method of introduction.

Caught up in my own excitement, I miss what was said between Skip and Billie. But the next line out of Skip's mouth is gold. I want to write it down, frame it, and hang it in the hallway.

"I really don't fucking know. I can't feel half my body right now and it's freaking me the fuck *out."*

Victory.

I refuse to look away as his legs buckle and half of his body collapses on top of Billie. My cheeks heat as a smile spreads wickedly across my face. Elation courses through my veins at unfathomable speeds. It's happening much quicker than I expected it would, all without a direct line to the bloodstream.

I obsess over the two of them with a new, heightened interest. Billie stares at Skip, her face flooded with worry. Meanwhile, Skip is lost in his own head and trying to figure out what exactly is happening to him. Or if it will stop. For a split-second, he looks up with this angered expression on his face—as if trying to project his hatred toward me.

Well, Little Skippy, project all you want. None of it will matter in about thirty seconds—give or take. When the time arrives, your brain will numb and you won't be able to formulate a genuine thought. So get it all out while you still can.

Not a second later, his arms slip out to the sides and his body drops. Simultaneously, Billie is hidden under his girth. *Yes!* Skip's face smashes against the side of Billie's face. His mouth just at her ear while his head traps her hair in place. This gets better with each passing second.

Not only will this be one of the most interesting deaths I have witnessed, but Billie will have the pleasure of experiencing every last breath Skip inhales. She reaches up and tries to free her hair from under his head. As soon as she yanks it free, the room goes silent.

Billie calls out to Skip. Asks him if he is okay. When he doesn't answer, she screams his name. Yet he still doesn't move. He doesn't flinch. He doesn't respond at all.

He's no longer breathing, but I know he's not clinically dead yet. That's not how the chemical works.

Right now, the chemical has created complete paralysis throughout his body. His organs are slowly failing as they shut down. It won't be long, though.

Billie makes a couple attempts to move Skip off her body. She finally manages to get out from under him, gives herself a minute to catch her breath, then bolts from the bed. She stares at his lifeless body with her arms wrapped around herself.

What is she thinking? What could possibly be going through that pesky little mind of hers?

She walks away from the bed, locates her underwear, and slips them on. She repeats the process when she retrieves her bra. After she latches the hooks in the back, she freezes. I lean in closer to the monitor, wondering what caught her attention.

And then I hear it.

The gurgle creeping up Skip's throat. The last moment of his life exiting his lungs. His body is officially dying in this very special moment.

Every millisecond I live in this moment, I soar high above the clouds.

Billie grabs his shoulders and shakes him with abandon. When she realizes his eyes and mouth still hang open, she pauses. As if she knows what this moment actually means. She shakes him again just as his body repeats the sound. She stops jostling him and listens as his body makes one last noise before it stills and ceases.

Her face pales as she falls to the floor, crawling into the closest corner and drawing her legs to her chest. Silently, she rocks herself into a stupor. She sits like this—in an upright fetal position—for several minutes. Obviously drowning in her head and trying to sort through how she feels. Trying to figure out how she could have saved him. Trying to figure out what she should do now.

Never fear, my little pretty, your time will come soon enough. No need to spend the last moments of your life worrying about poor, sex fanatic Skip. Surely, if the roles were reversed and you died on the bed, he wouldn't be crying in the corner. To be honest, I think he would try to get out of the room as quickly as possible and pretend like he knew nothing about what happened to you.

This is what you should be thinking about. He wouldn't give a damn about your pathetic little life. Just like I don't give a damn about your pathetic little life. Which is the exact reason why you've been alone for so long. Because no one gave a damn. Because you practically whored yourself at the bar every night and sang your stupid karaoke music. All for attention and alcohol.

A noise snaps me out of my reverie and I gaze at Billie as she balls up her fingers and beats her own fist into the side of her head.

She's angry with herself.

She starts prattling on about being sorry and directing

the apology to the dead body on the bed. She continually apologizes to Skip and tells his lifeless meat suit she is to blame for his death.

No, sweetheart. Skip is the only one at fault in this instance. Lo and behold, you are all responsible for your own demise. I am simply the catalyst helping you reach the goal. This is my job. My passion. To help rid the world of the scum. The people who think they are above living life the dignified way.

I regulate them.

I reign them in.

I teach them the ultimate lesson.

I teach them their actions will now result in a consequence.

The ultimate consequence.

I reach down on the seat cushion beside me and pick up the figurine. Holding it in front of me, I examine the features of the cold doll.

A squared porcelain face. Short, salt-and-pepper hair. Blue dress pants. A light blue button-up dress shirt. Brown dress shoes.

As I hold the doll in my hands, I rotate it from side to side and view it from different angles. True perfection. Now I will have another masterpiece to add to my collection. I bring the doll up to my face so that it butts its nose against mine.

"Can't wait to put you on the shelf, Little Skippy."

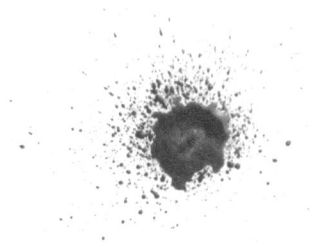

BILLIE

I have sat on this cold, scratchy wood for a while now. Probably mere minutes, but it seems as if hours have passed. That is the interesting fact about fear, it changes your perception with the snap of a finger. It would serve me right if I died in this very corner—petrifying into the woman who couldn't resist the attention of a wanton man.

I deserve it.

I stop rocking. My butt cheeks are cold and sore from the obsessive motion against the hard floor. Peering up from my knees, I take another glance at Skip on the bed. His body still in the same position—frozen in place on his stomach with his arms outstretched and his face angled to the right.

What am I supposed to do with his body? Should I leave it here? Can't exactly take him outside and bury him.

If I left him on the bed and abandoned the room, does that make me an asshole? Again.

But how easy would it be to walk out of this room, join the others, and pretend like I have no clue he is lying dead as a doornail on the bed in the back bedroom? It is one-hundred percent doable.

Although the option seems the most coldhearted, it's more than likely the best option. But how exactly do I move forward? The moment I walk out there, the moment I am surrounded by the others in the house, they will hound me with question after question. They will ask what we were doing back here? Surely, one of them will ask where Skip is.

Will I be able to maintain a poker face throughout their interrogation?

Can I lie to them? Tell them he was tired and wanted to sleep a while.

Would they believe the lie I dish out? Would they fall so easily for the fabrication?

The worst possible question of them all… would they want details of what happened? Between me and Skip.

My feet pivot in place—toes tap the floor, lift as my heels rock back, then glide forward again—as I seesaw my body weight back and forth. Divulging what happened in this room is far from desirable. Not as if I have never bragged about sexual partners with friends before. But these women were not my friends. The same rules didn't apply here. One—the women beyond these walls… they think less of me. Two—I have never dealt with death before. Not like this anyway.

No. I couldn't—wouldn't—share anything that happened in this room. If any of them says anything nasty or harasses me, I will simply walk away. Separate myself from them. I am strong enough.

I got this. I can pretend as if nothing happened. Nothing

bad, at least. This is not the first time I have had to do the walk of shame. Although, this is a wholly different form of shame.

Extending my legs out in front of me, I rub life back into my calves and feet. After I regain some form of circulation in them, I crawl onto my hands and knees before planting my feet on the floor and pushing myself upright. Standing in place, I shake out my limbs and stretch my upper body.

Once I feel capable of walking without falling, I amble over to the bed and take one last glimpse at Skip. His skin seems paler already, which is odd. I thought noticeable changes took hours. Yes, I have been sitting in the corner for a while, but it hasn't been that long. Has it?

In this house, everything feels off. Wrong. Different. What feels like an hour is probably somewhat closer to ten minutes. The energy is peculiar. Walls and furniture and various trinkets change in the blink of an eye. This whole place is one huge, repetitive nightmare. A nightmare I wish would end.

I step back and scan the room, looking for the rest of my clothes. My shirt lays on the floor near the bed. I walk over, snatch it up, and slip it over my head. On the opposite side of the bed, I spot my jeans.

Once dressed, I slip on my shoes. I comb my fingers through my hair and wince as they get caught on countless knots. Earlier, I remember seeing a hairbrush on the dresser —one of the many *conveniences* this house seems to be loaded with.

Just like the condom.

I shake my head and vanquish the path my thoughts

were headed down. The past cannot be changed, so why dwell. Picking up the brush, I ignore the fact it appears brand new and unused. Running the bristles through my hair, I close my eyes and picture myself in my bedroom at home. Combing the brush through the strands over and over, I don't want to leave this temporary moment of normalcy.

Alas, every moment has its end.

When I open my eyes, I find I'm still in the same exact nightmare. If only it were so simple—to just close your eyes, reset your mind, and when you reopen them, you are exactly where you want to be.

But this is my own personal hell, and that is definitely not the hand I have been dealt. In my short time here, I have come to accept this. My fate. Everything happens for a reason, they say. Perhaps this place is some form of justice for all the wrongs I have done. All the things I have swept under the rug.

Like this.

Like redressing and making myself look appropriate, so I can leave this room and go into the next. And in that other room, I will sit in a chair beside five other people and pretend Skip isn't lying naked on this bed... dead.

Just one more tick mark on my list of horrible life choices. But, at this point in my life, I have grown to accept the result. There is nothing I can do to change what happens. There is nothing I can do to change fate.

If this is hell, I might as well look good as I burn for my sins. If this is hell... what does it matter if I continue down the same path. My fate is sealed. There is no going back.

But one question still remains.

If this is my hell, who are all of these other people?

I have no clue who they are. Have never seen them a day in my life. Or them me, for that matter. So why were we all sandwiched in this place together?

Not sure how I will learn the answer, but I sure as hell won't be getting any answers standing in this room.

Step by step, I stroll across the room to the door. I wrap my hand around the doorknob and stand tall. Taking a deep breath, I pray to keep a straight face while I spew my bullshit reasons for being in this room for so long.

Then I exhale and turn the knob.

CHAPTER SEVEN

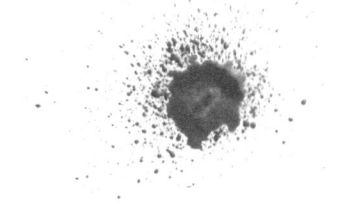

MAKING her way to the door, Billie extended a hand and took hold of the knob. She paused for a beat and inhaled deeply before twisting the knob and tugging the door open. But the door didn't budge. Billie gave it another twist and yank and met the same result.

But her stubborn nature, and the fact that Skip laid dead mere feet away, didn't let her quit so easily.

The handle rattled in her grip as she continually twisted it left and right, over and over. Then she wrenched it with a bit more force. Put all her weight into the task. And yet, the door remained sealed.

Frustrated, her hands dropped to her sides as she tipped her head back and huffed. "Please," she begged toward the ceiling. "Please, just let me leave." She tried the knob again. Nothing.

Rather than give up and sulk, Billie balled her fingers into tight fists and lifted them. Not a breath later, her fists beat against the wood like a toddler throwing a tantrum. Each time flesh met wood, she screamed. A mix of irritated grunts and hollers to the women down the hall.

They have to hear me, right? Billie thought this each time her hands hit the grain. Each time she screamed for someone to come and help her. She no longer cared if one of them discovered Skip was dead in the room.

But when she heard no response, when no one came to her rescue, she surrendered to her fate. Being stuck in the room with a man who would still be alive if not for her. *Thump.* Her head fell forward and smacked against the door. Defeat consumed Billie as her chest heaved. She didn't *want* to give up, but remained rooted in place, fists tight at her sides.

Resigned to give it one last-ditch effort, she lifted her head and adjusted her posture. Standing taller, she reached for the doorknob one last time and gave it a twist.

This time, her efforts are rewarded as the door opened in her direction. An audible exhale floated through the air as she stepped forward and exited the room. Before shutting the door behind her, she turned briefly and took one last glance at Skip's frigid body.

Could she really do this? Could she just leave him dead and exposed on the bed?

Then she faced forward and closed the door behind her. Took a deep breath, smoothed her clothes, and continued on as if everything were normal.

Standing on the opposite side of the door had its own form of relief. Comfort.

In the hall, Billie relaxed more. Her shoulders sagged. Her body lost some of its rigidity.

Pressing her hand to the center of the door, Billie apologized one last time to the man on the other side. Apologized for doing whatever necessary to survive.

"I'm just sorry, Skip. Hope you can forgive me."

When she finally lifted her head and faced the open end of the hallway, she noted several differences in the appearance. If possible, the hall was longer.

What was once maybe fifteen feet, now seemed almost double.

The walls—once peeling apart—were now immaculate and littered with several framed images, floor to ceiling. Billie crept forward a couple steps and honed in on one of the eye level photos.

Billie sucked in a sharp breath and hissed. One of her hands flew up and covered her mouth as she inched away from the image.

A chill settled over her skin as she paled. She mumbled soft words of disbelief.

"I-It can't be." She shook her head. *"No... it simply cannot be."*

Unable to look away, she stepped up to the image again. Without a second thought, Billie reached out, gripped the edges of the frame, and removed it from the wall. She studied it with vigorous intent, turning it left and right and hoping she was imagining things.

"How?"

Inches from her face, Billie squinted at the photo. When the reality of it hit her, she stiffened. In her hands was an image of Skip. His lifeless body lying atop hers.

The frame dropped to the floor. Glass shattered. Shards

spraying in every direction. Billie stumbled back until she clashed with the wall.

Hands clasped over her mouth, she faced left then right, checking up and down both ends of the hall. Her head shook nonstop. Brows furrowed in disbelief. Breath ragged from shock.

"Is anyone there? Hello?"

She faced the dead end of the hall, the narrow space darker the farther it extended.

A voice bounced off the walls in the hall. Rather than turn and run, it prompted Billie to slowly put one foot in front of the other and follow the sound farther into the darkness. The need to fulfill her curiosity superseding her own safety. After all, the photo from the wall—now under a mound of glass shards—indicated someone else was nearby. Someone else knew Skip was dead.

"What was that? Couldn't hear you."

The voice echoed down the corridor again. Words garbled and luring her in further. Billie called out again, asking whoever was there to repeat themselves. That she couldn't hear them clearly.

This time, when the voice spoke up, she heard every word clear as day.

"I hope you enjoyed your time with Little Skippy... because he'll be the last person you'll ever speak to face-to-face."

Stock-still in the darkness, her eyes widened as her breathing spiked. She slammed her eyes shut and flattened her palms against the wall as she settled her breathing. A moment later, she opened her eyes and nodded. Without a second thought, Billie spun around, faced the open end of the hall, and ran.

Fear motivated Billie to escape as adrenaline coursed through her bloodstream. She didn't know who the voice belonged to, but she had no intention of finding out.

As she approached the end of the hall, a crackling erupted around her. In the blink of an eye, the walls changed. Before her foot hit the ground, the hallway transformed. Grew longer. The open end as far away as when she started for it.

Not wanting to give up, Billie ran for the dining room on the other end. But running seemed to get her nowhere. Literally. With every other stride Billie took, the hallway grew longer and longer.

Suddenly, the hallway turned into a never-ending treadmill. She ran for her life and got nowhere in the process. The proverbial carrot dangled in front of her, but was seemingly impossible to catch.

Billie's pulse pounded a vicious rhythm behind her ribcage. A white noise thrummed loudly in her ears. Legitimate fear trickled in her veins. She wanted to scream, but her throat scraped the air like sandpaper. Swallowing, she yelled for help. Her voice hoarse and winded, but she hoped someone would hear her and run to her rescue.

The farther she ran, the more her calves burned. The more her lungs begged for mercy. And the more she considered this may never end.

Minutes passed and no one responded to her cries for help. No one came bolting around the corner to rescue her. Not a single soul.

She didn't want to give in so easily. Didn't want to surrender to the person who tortured her with mind games. So she screamed again. And again. She continued screaming for what felt like days while she ran toward her potential escape.

Billie ran in the dim-lit hall—the end constantly in her line of sight and always just out of reach. Hissing, she slowed to a stop, grabbed her waist, and squeezed her sides. A stabbing pain erupted beneath the right side of her ribcage. Fatigue and dehydration weighed down on her and halted her running. The cramp in her side eliciting jab after jab.

Bent at the waist, Billie spent a moment settling her heart rate and breathing. Hands on her knees, she inhaled slow and steady breaths. Once her body regulated, she peered up and saw the end of the hall. Just feet away was one of the women. Less than ten feet, maybe. Billie yelled for her. Called out all the names from her memory bank.

But no one stepped any closer. No one responded or glanced her way.

Instead of running, Billie opted to walk toward the open end. This time, the hallway didn't move with her. This time, the space allowed her to walk toward the end.

As she approached the open end of the hall, she saw two of the women—Kelly and Nina. They chatted not far from the dining table. Billie smiled as hope flooded her. She had made it. She finally got to the end and would be free from the twisted mind game.

Thank god.

But as quickly as hope arrived, it vanished. In two short

strides, Billie slammed face-first into an invisible wall. She stumbled back a step, but regained her footing. Billie pressed her hands to the air at the sides of her face. A foot in front of her, her palms slapped the air as if it were solid. As if it were a concrete wall.

"Hey! Can you hear me?" Billie yelled as she banged her hands against the force field blocking her. She got zero reactions from the others. Even though Kelly and Nina stood an arm's reach away, they couldn't see Billie. Couldn't hear her. Couldn't help her.

Then the hall shifted again.

And before her heart beat once, Billie was suddenly back in the middle of the long corridor. Back where she started.

She briskly walked toward the open room. The hall spinning like a treadmill once more. Within seconds, Billie sprinted full force in place.

Picking up her stride, she felt closer to the end. Hope surged in her once more as she pushed herself a little harder. Then, a strange mechanical sound squealed. Cranks groaned on either side of her. But she couldn't see the source.

The screech caused a new bout of adrenaline to erupt in her body. With each breath she took, the noise grew louder and louder. When the mechanical sound screeched as if right on top of her, she peeked over her shoulder to investigate, but saw nothing.

Then she faced forward…

A sharp, wire-thin piece of metal slid down and stretched across the width of the hall. Before she had time to stop, her neck collided with the metal. Her head fell behind her as the momentum of her legs carried the rest of her headless body forward. One step later, her lifeless body hit the floor. A loud thump echoed down the hall and into the next room.

Blood pumped from Billie's arteries and pooled around her decapitated form.

Kelly stepped closer to the opening of the hall and scanned the corridor. But there was nothing there. Nothing visible past the invisible barrier between her and Billie anyway. As Kelly stepped away, she called out to the others.

"Not sure what that was. Maybe it's the headboard banging against the wall." Then Kelly joined the others, laughed a moment, and they resumed their previous conversation.

CHAPTER EIGHT

JENNIFER

A GRUMBLE ERUPTS from my stomach and I'd swear everyone within ten feet hears it. Kristen dumps can after can of chicken into the huge pot on the stove. A delicious aroma wafts in the air and has my mouth salivating. I want to wait until she finishes cooking the chicken and dumplings, but I don't know if I'll be able to wait much longer. My stomach may eat itself if I don't feed it soon.

That infamous line from *Little Shop of Horrors* jogs through my head as my stomach gurgles again.

"Now we just need to let it simmer on the stove for twenty to thirty minutes and then we can add the dumplings," Kristen states matter-of-factly as she grabs a large wooden spoon and stirs the concoction.

Twenty to thirty minutes? I don't know if I can wait that long. Any minute now, I'll probably collapse or pass out.

The five of us stand around the spacious kitchen and stare at one another as if we are unsure what to do next. Kristen suggests we clean up the dirty dishes and wipe down the counters. With not many dishes to clean and very little on the counter, we clear the mess up quickly.

Not sure what to do afterward, we decide to settle in the living room and wait for the timer to go off.

Everyone gossips all things Skip and Billie. Each of us intrigued by what is happening in the room at the end of the hall. As fascinating as it is, I zone out during the conversation.

My stomach groans in anger again, louder than before, and I wrap my arms around my midsection. Belinda glances my way. I tap my stomach and apologize for interrupting the chat. Belinda simply laughs at me and carries on talking with the others.

A few minutes pass and the chatter continues. At some point while I was zoned out, the conversation has transitioned from Billie and Skip to television shows and what each of them has been binge-watching.

My stomach protests at my ignoring it. At this rate, I am certain it will eat my other organs if I don't give it actual food soon. How much longer will my body deal with the loss of food? To my recollection, I have never gone this long without eating. And I have no idea how long we have been in this house. A few hours? Half a day? A day or more? Feels like days.

How long has it been since we left the kitchen? Shouldn't the buzzer be blaring already? Another angry growl belts out from my belly. I press a fist into my midsection and try to quiet it.

"Hey, sorry to interrupt. How long do the dumplings need to cook? You know, once the soup part is done."

"Maybe another ten or fifteen minutes," Kristen shares, unfazed by my noisy stomach.

Ten or fifteen minutes. Not sure I will last that long.

I rise from the couch and head back to the kitchen, determined to find something that will hold me over until the chicken and dumplings is done. Just something small. Cheese crackers or a granola bar. Maybe pretzels or peanuts.

Stepping into the kitchen, I stare blankly at the cabinet doors.

I have no clue where anything is, let alone my options. Guess I open one cabinet at a time and work my way down the line. One of these cabinets is bound to have *something* that will satisfy my hunger. Even if temporarily.

The first cabinet door I open is jam-packed with canned goods. There has to be at least a hundred or more cans in this cabinet. Honestly, I am surprised the cabinet hasn't fallen from the wall.

Loaded with every possible canned vegetable on the market—check. Every version of canned fruit—some of which I have never heard of before—check. Various types of canned fish, chicken, and ham—check, check, and check. Never have I seen so many canned items—other than on the supermarket shelves—in my life. This place is like a doomsday shelter.

Closing the door, I move on to the next cabinet.

The next is equally packed. Artfully stacked boxes of pasta, rice in various flavors and types, boxed potatoes, macaroni and cheese, and jarred sauces to accompany them. I contemplate the ramen noodles, but pass.

When I open the next door, I smile so wide a pain shoots from the corners of my mouth to my ears. My heart beats a little faster as I stare at my own slice of heaven.

On the left side of the bottom shelf is three oversized jars of peanut butter—smooth, not crunchy. *Thank god.* Some off-brand I have never seen, but right now I give zero fucks. To the right of the peanut butter is three equally large jars of jelly and preserves—grape, strawberry, and raspberry (my absolute favorite).

Snatching a jar of the creamy nut spread and sweet fruity preserves, I set them on the counter while I hunt down bread or crackers. Scouring through the remaining food cabinets, my efforts end unsuccessfully. I slump against the counter, crestfallen. My high hopes of eating a peanut butter and jelly sandwich slowly plummet down, down, down.

Then a memory flickers to life in my head. I walk over to the fridge and mentally cross my fingers.

I once lived with a roommate who always stashed the bread in the fridge or freezer. She swore it stayed fresher longer if you did. As I reach for the fridge handle, I say a prayer to the sandwich gods, begging them for just two slices of bread.

The door swings open and I scan the abundance of food inside. As soon as my eyes land on the prize, fireworks explode in my chest.

Smack dab in front of me, dead center, is a loaf of my favorite white bread. Again, I am beyond thankful it is another style I prefer. Don't really care for those seedy breads.

Riffling through the fridge, I finagle the bread out and walk back to my sandwich station.

As I remove bread from the bag, Kristen enters the kitchen and throws me the motherly stink-eye. She picks up the wooden spoon and stirs the chicken soup mixture, leaving a little on the spoon and bringing it to her mouth to taste.

She closes her eyes and tips her head side to side. A small moan of pleasure rumbles in her throat. My mind goes straight to the gutter and I want to ask if her foodgasm was good. But I don't.

"If you didn't like chicken and dumplings, all you had to do was say something. I would've made you something different," she says. Her tone is soft. Gentle. And I suddenly have the urge to apologize. Kristen is obviously a people pleaser, and I stomped on her meal plans.

"Thanks. Actually, I love chicken and dumplings. But my stomach doesn't seem to have any patience. Feels as if it's going to eat my insides any minute. Remember the Venus flytrap in *Little Shop of Horrors*? That's what's happening here." I point to my stomach. "Figured I'd make a sandwich to calm the beast and then have some of the chicken and dumplings when it's ready."

Kristen lights up and relaxes simultaneously. "Gotcha. Well, I'm adding the dumplings in a few more minutes. And then we only have to wait for them to cook. Which won't take long. Ten to fifteen was a stretch." She stirs the soup again, then stops. Her eyes widen. "Ooh... I just thought of something to have with the soup."

Her enthusiasm has my stomach singing with excitement. "And what would that be?" I ask as I open drawers and hunt for a knife. After opening the third drawer with no luck, Kristen pulls out a drawer, retrieves a knife, and hands it to me. "Thanks."

"Sure thing. Seeing you with the bread sparked the idea of garlic and herb bread to go with the chicken and dumplings. I'll grab the baguette in the freezer."

Kristen retrieves the long, thin loaf from the freezer and sets it on the counter. "Should be able to cut it up easily in a few minutes."

I ask where the plates are and Kristen points me in the right direction. Fetching a plate, I return to my setup and assemble my sandwich.

Cracking open the jar of peanut butter, I peel back the seal and bring the jar to my nose. I inhale deeply as my eyes roll back into my head. *God, I love peanut butter.*

Immediately, I get to work on my sandwich. I slather on a thick layer of peanut butter, followed by a large helping of preserves.

Since the age of five, I always made my peanut butter and jelly the exact same way. White bread. A hefty layer of peanut butter on the left slice. I wipe the knife on the right slice to clean it off. Then saturate the right slice in jelly. The two slices get pressed firmly together and cut into four triangles.

Always.

When I finish with the preserves, I lick the knife clean. I pick up the slices, hold them side by side, then slap them together. When the slices line up, I set the sandwich back on the plate, grab the knife, and cut it in triangles.

Perfect as always.

I glance over at Kristen, who drops the first few dumplings into the pot before grabbing more. A growl bellows from my stomach. Glad I chose not to wait. Picking up the first triangle, I feed the beast in my belly.

As soon as the sweet and savory concoction hits my tongue, bliss courses through my veins.

Thank you, sandwich gods.

CHAPTER NINE

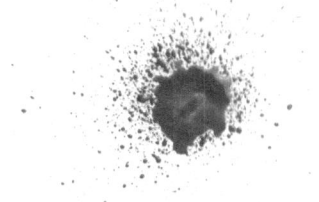

JENNIFER CUT her sandwich in a manner most children generally enjoyed—corner to corner in four small triangles. Kristen busied herself at the stove, adding the mountain of dumplings into the pot one at a time. The soup mixture splattered as each square of dough hit the steamy liquid. With each plop, Kristen pressed her lips in a flat line and flinched as if she feared being burned.

Once all the dumplings were deposited in the large pot, Kristen picked the spoon up from the counter and ladled some of the thick, creamy broth over each dumpling. After coating them, she lidded the pot and returned to where the baguette loaf thawed on the counter.

Kristen glanced at Jennifer as she finished the first triangle of her sandwich. "Should I make the garlic bread thinner, thicker, or average slices? Or it doesn't matter?"

"Thick would be best," Jennifer mumbled past her squirrel-packed cheeks.

"You could've waited until you finished chewing. Patience is my middle name."

Jennifer shrugged, a cheeky smile tugging at her lips. "Sorry."

Kristen shook her head. Opening a drawer, she retrieved a bread knife, then grabbed the cutting board and got to work on the baguette.

Kristen cut the loaf into angled slices and spread them out when finished. She left the bread to thaw for a couple more minutes while checking on the dumplings. Lifting the lid, she gently stirred the concoction before flipping each dumpling and spooning the soup over top once more.

From the fridge, Kristen fetched an oversized tub of butter and set it down beside the bread. Then, she went to a cabinet stockpiled with spices and herbs. Kristen sifted through the jars until she located the perfect seasonings for the bread.

While Kristen got to work on the bread, Jennifer finished chewing the second triangle of her sandwich. Waiting until she swallowed the last of her bite, Jennifer asked if Kristen needed assistance.

"No, I'm good. You finish eating so you'll be done by the time everything else is ready," Kristen said.

Jennifer nodded then hoisted herself on to the counter and grabbed the third section of her sandwich. She nibbled at the edges, biting off the crust first and eating the sandwich as if a child. She was off in her own world, licking at the preserves squirting out the opposite side. Kristen buttered and seasoned the bread slices.

Once done, Kristen turned on the oven, but hesitated setting the temperature. She glanced over her shoulder at the toaster oven. After momentary contemplation, Kristen decided the toaster oven would be the better option and turned off the range oven. It would be less mess and cook the garlic bread quicker.

As Kristen turned on the toaster oven, she spotted the cord laid unplugged on the counter. Picking it up, she plugged it in a nearby outlet and set the temperature. While it heated up, Kristen retrieved two small trays and loaded the first round of bread on the pans.

As Kristin added the last slice on the pan, Jennifer swallowed the first bite of her last triangle then waved at Kristen. "Hey. I think something's wrong with the toaster oven." Her sandwich hand pointed toward the mini oven.

Kristen glanced over and saw the bottom heating element flicker as if someone flipped a switch every other second. She walked back over and adjusted the temperature dial, testing to see if lowering the temperature would make a difference.

For a moment, the heating elements remained on. So, Kristen walked off to check on the soup. A few steps away, Jennifer grunted—her cheeks puffed like a squirrel with too much in its muzzle—and pointed to the toaster oven.

Hands on her hips, Kristen halted in her tracks. "What the heck? Thought the toaster oven would be easier, but maybe I should've used the regular oven after all. I'll set the oven and unplug that stupid thing."

Kristen shook her head, walked to the stove, checked the chicken and dumplings, then set the oven. She took out a couple larger pans and transferred the bread on them, adding the remaining slices from the cutting board.

She reached the toaster oven, wrapped her fingers

around the cord, and slid them up until she reached the plug. As soon as she tugged the wire from the wall, her body went rigid. Stock-still. Convulsing. Twitching. Rocking where she stood.

Jennifer jumped off the counter and bolted over to Kristen. Kristen's eyes bulged from the sockets. Pupils fully dilated as the whites reddened more and more with each passing second.

Jennifer yelled for someone to come help her in the kitchen.

Jennifer pinched her nose with her fingers as a horrid stench floated through the air. And that was the moment she noticed Kristen's hair fraying. The whites of her eyes almost fully red as the burning smell grew more pronounced and unavoidable.

Jennifer screamed at the horror happening in front of her. "What can I do?" She stared wide-eyed at Kristen, hands hovering inches away, wanting to help but also not wanting to touch her. Unsure of how to help without injuring herself.

Taking a moment to mentally step outside the situation, Jennifer thought about the safety procedures taught to her at the lab. Remembered someone mentioning rubber. Rubber grounded you from the electric shock.

Instantly, she yanked open every drawer in search of anything made of rubber.

After the last drawer, defeat registered on her face. Nothing.

She watched as Kristen's body continued to shudder violently. Jennifer clutched at her chest as her own heart rioted against the horror scene. A thin veil of smoke billowed from Kristen's body. Burn marks singed patches of her skin as she gripped the cord in the wall.

Jennifer opened a drawer full of kitchen hand towels and took several out. Tying them together, she tossed the length over Kristen's shoulders and yanked her body away from the outlet.

Kristen fell to the floor as Jennifer crawled to her side, but keeping her hands clear. "Hey, Kristen. Can you hear me? Are you okay?" She shifted angles to get Kristen's attention, but got no response.

Her body laid stiff. Skin charred and peeling. Hair whiter and frizzy and sizzling.

Jennifer tested touching her with a single finger. Once she realized the possibility of Kristen electrocuting her passed, Jennifer flipped Kristen over on her back. She dug her heels in the floor, scooted back, and threw her hand over her mouth. Her sandwich on the cusp of a reappearance.

Blisters marred Kristen's forehead, cheekbones, and ears. Her hair ghostly and crisp. Eyes melted in the sockets. Lips bubbled and husking. Brows and lashes practically non-existent.

Less than a minute passed between the time Kristen tugged on the cord and when Jennifer released her grip. In the blink of an eye, Kristen went from cooking dinner for a group of strangers to electrocuted on the kitchen floor in a strange house.

Three down. Four to go.

CHAPTER TEN

JENNIFER

My FEET continually push off the floor in front of me as I try to scoot myself farther away from Kristen. But I can't get away. Not with my back flush to the wall.

Her ashy, burned flesh smokes right before my eyes. The most vile, putrid aroma wafts up my nose and fills every corner of the room. And I will never forget this moment. Her crisped flesh and smoky skin scent will be forever etched into my memory.

I close my eyes and all I see is Kristen. Her body thrashing violently as she held on to that cord and her existence was electrocuted into dust. The sizzling replays in my ears of her skin and hair and nails frying as if a potato thrown in hot oil. The pungent odor her skin elicited permanently clings to the hair follicles inside my nasal cavity. A constant reminder of the atrocious death I bore witness.

This will torture me for years to come. Not just Kristen being fried like a Snickers bar at a carnival, but this whole place. There is no possible way I will forget. No way in hell. Who knows if I will ever sleep again.

Somehow, I scramble to my feet and stand, leaning on the counter for support.

Closing my eyes, I inhale deeply and brace myself for what happens next. I allow myself this single moment to breathe and gather my composure. Once I settle as much as feasible, I straighten my spine and take one last look at Kristen. Then, I walk out of the kitchen quickly and go in search of the others.

"Kelly? Nina? Belinda? Where are you guys? I need help."

I step into the dining room and something is different—off. *Is this the same room?*

The table in the dining room is no longer the lengthy, wooden table with matching chairs. I stare at the table and blink several times, wondering if I have become delusional. Or did watching someone get electrocuted mess with my head? Either way, this is one vivid, fucked-up nightmare. The type where you feel awake, but aren't actually sure.

As bizarre as everything has been here, I can't grasp how any of this could be real. It is too fucked-up.

The table which could have easily sat ten has vanished into thin air. In its place is a smaller, square table. A black metal frame and legs for the base with a thick glass pane settled on top. Four chairs with plush white cushions on the seat. A black vase sits in the center of the table with dozens of red roses.

"Weird," I mumble to myself.

Can't say I have seen roses such a deep shade of red.

A red so rich it resembles blood.

My stomach churns as nausea claws its way up my throat and consumes every square inch of my torso.

I hate puking. Have spent my entire life forcing myself not to vomit every time the occasion arises. Everything about it is foul. And it is a never-ending cycle of sickness. Convulse, heave, smell it, repeat.

No matter the cost, I work to keep my stomach at bay. Unsure if what happened to Kristen has it in knots. Or if it's the sandwich. Maybe both. Either way, I've got this.

I continue in search of the others and head for the living room. When I step through the archway, I notice the living room has also changed. Again. The walls now coated with khaki-colored paint. Sporadic dark splotches splattered along the expanse. The couch and love seat from fifteen minutes ago… gone. Replaced with an L-shaped, black leather sectional swallowing the space.

What the fuck is this place?

"Hello?" I call out, hoping someone will respond. "Nina? Belinda? Kelly? Where are you?" A chill ricochets up my spine when no one answers.

I walk the perimeter of the room and stop in front of the window. The yellow film previously coating the glass is no longer present and I can see beyond the walls of this hellhole. Out in the world where life moves on.

The sun shines brightly above the house. I stare outside a moment and zone out. A sense of loss seeps into my bloodstream and overwhelms me. Devours me and leaves me momentarily breathless.

Not as if I laid out in the sunlight regularly. But being kept from something makes you crave it more. Makes you yearn for those lost picnics or hiking days. Days when you dug your toes into the warmed earth.

With where the sun rests in the sky, I'd guess it's probably near two or three in the afternoon. Opposite the glass, black bars butt against the windowpane and remind me of the prison sentence I somehow inherited. Beyond the window, several tall trees line a small path leading to the porch. The porch is average in size and has a small table between two Adirondack chairs.

A memory of the last time I stood in this room pops up and I step away from the window. I peer around the room and curiosity strikes like a mallet hitting a gong.

Weren't there two windows before? How in the hell is there only one now?

This place is some twisted, haunted house nightmare. A place where horror junkies get their rocks off. Some sick, twisted fuck's version of a good time.

I left the room for fifteen minutes—tops—and it quietly morphed into a whole new structure. How the fuck is that even possible? Logically, it makes zero sense. And where the hell did everyone else go?

Needing to get out of this version of the *Twilight Zone*, I head back to the dining room and walk past the table, toward the hallway. A few feet from the table, I realize the walls in the dining room are different. Shifted. Where the kitchen was once open to the dining room, it isn't any longer. The bar top counter between the two rooms has magically vanished. And the entrance to the hallway? Gone. There is no hallway.

The walls resembled a house of mirrors... except there

were no mirrors. Every time I acclimated to my surroundings, they changed. Surely, some douchebag was getting their jollies at watching our constant state of confusion.

The dining room wall—opposite the living room—was now longer. The entire room more spacious. On the wall where the hallway used to be is three doors—the center one open. I inched closer to see inside without stepping in. From ten feet away, the white interior sparkled. White tile on the walls and floors. A white toilet and an oversized white clawfoot bathtub.

One of the most pristine and beautiful bathrooms I had ever seen. If one dubbed a bathroom beautiful.

The doors to either side of the bathroom... bolted with the same industrial-strength locks as the front door.

Are the others locked in those rooms? It is next to impossible for me to open them, but maybe they can... if they're on the other side.

My stomach gurgles, but I ignore the discomfort growing in my belly. Staring at the closed doors for a beat, I go to the left first. Stepping up to the door, I say a silent prayer one of them is on the opposite side and is okay. I curl my fingers into fists and bang them against the grain.

"Hey? Anyone in there? Guys? I could use your help out here."

I pause when the sides of my hands ache. I cup my ear to the door and listen. Hoping to hear one of them cry out or kick. Anything.

But there is no response.

So, I bang on the door a second time. As more time passes and no one responds, the small sliver of hope in my chest fades. The optimist inside me wants to believe maybe they aren't in this room. That they're safe somewhere else. Maybe in the other room.

But how would they have gotten there in the first place?

What an asinine question considering where we are. Considering how none of us remember coming to this place.

Reluctantly, I step away from door one and go to the other. Crossing my fingers, I go through the motions of banging on this door.

A hollowness grows tenfold in my chest. Not a peep or a yell or a bang is heard from the other side. I don't understand. Where the hell are they? Three people couldn't just vanish into thin air. Can they? They have to be somewhere in the house.

Maybe they are trapped in the hall, banging on the wall to find me.

Or perhaps they ran into the kitchen while I stared out the window.

I head back toward the kitchen and round the corner that wasn't previously there. Kristen's body lies on the floor. There is no sign of Belinda, Kelly or Nina.

I slump in place and hang my head as confusion infiltrates and exhausts me. I want to find everyone else, but I haven't the slightest idea where to look. I'm running out of options.

I don't want to give up, but what else can I do? And what the hell do I do with Kristen's body?

Leaving her on the floor seems wrong.

I wander back to the living room and scan the shelves

on the wall opposite the window in search of a blanket. Before the room changed—for the second time—I remember seeing a blanket when we picked up the puzzle. Now, it's just a matter of figuring out where it got relocated. Or if it is still here.

Pulling a brown wicker basket off the shelf, I discover a fluffy, blue blanket and haul it from the basket. Hugging it in my arms, I walk back to the kitchen. But this time when I round the kitchen corner, I skid to a halt. Shake my head in disbelief and take a step back. My eyes widen in shock and I blink several times.

This can't be real. Can't be. I don't believe my eyes. They must be playing more tricks on me. Must be. What the fuck is going on?

The kitchen floor is bare. Kristen's body… vanished. Absent. As if it were never there in the first place. As if the tragedy of her being electrocuted for a minute plus never existed.

I close my eyes and the images of her death flash behind my lids. She was here. In the very spot I stand. She was here.

How do people disappear so easily? Without a sound. Or a trace of evidence.

My head swims in the possibility I most definitely am not alone. And it isn't the three other women who make me feel this way. Someone else is here. In the walls, perhaps. More than likely, behind the industrial locked doors.

I slowly back out of the room and head for the living room, plopping down on the couch and curling the blanket between my chest and lap.

My stomach roils. The knots twisting tighter with everything happening.

Where is everyone else? Am I the only person here? The notion seems impossible and is unsettling.

"Hello… can *anyone* hear me?"

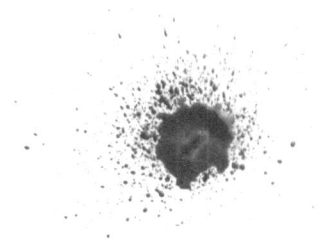

CAPTOR

Look at her. Sitting on the couch curled in on herself. Hugging the blanket like a goddamn adolescent. "Poor little baby probably needs mommy to make her feel better. Boo-fucking-hoo."

Seeing Jennifer on the monitor, scared and helpless and weeping like a child, makes my pulse thunder and blood hum with the thrill. Before each death, a buzz throttles throughout me. Lifts me higher and higher. It's almost as if someone took all the good side effects of each drug and blended them together.

Pure fucking euphoria.

I love how easily I trick this one. Her mind so gullible, but in a different way from the others. With a couple flicks of a switch, she believes she has been transported somewhere new. She sees objects in the shapes and forms and sizes I *want* her to see.

And I present them with illusions of grandeur. I limit their access and put them where I want them.

If they only knew what this house truly looked like. Stains and excrement and undiluted filth. None of them would touch any surface if they got an actual glimpse. If anything, they would crawl out of their skin.

But this house has been in my family for generations. Seven generations to be exact. Nearly two hundred years of history reside in these walls. Generations of farmers and pioneers. Witches and specters. The house sits on a large plot of land—most of the open property behind the house. Mostly wooded. And lucky for me, the second generation created a family cemetery on the land.

Never seems suspicious if I dig holes back there.

Since the responsibility of the home fell into my hands, I have maintained the exterior. Kept the siding and paint and trim up-to-date and modern. The grassy area surrounding the house is mowed and the plants are pristine and perfectly manicured. Anyone gazing at the exterior would never suspect the truth captured within the walls.

But there are reasons I don't change the interior. Reasons why it isn't as *pleasant* as the outside.

If you think about everything that happens in these walls, the house would need constant bleaching. Why bother. Why go through so much work, just to repeat the process again and again.

The only valuable objects inside these walls are the artificial intelligence components I have installed. Spread throughout each room and hidden from the naked eye. The AI allows me to manipulate my victims. Make them see what *I* want them to see. So, if I want them to believe they're standing in opulence, they believe it.

To my right, in a plush armchair, is a stack of "small occupants". I call these occupants my… souvenirs. Yes. Souvenir is the perfect descriptor. And I have a souvenir for each of the seven. One for each I have the pleasure of watching perish.

My souvenirs.

As of now, three pristine, lifelike replicas of Skip, Billie, and Kristen sit in the armchair. My sweet little souvenirs won't wait much longer before a new playmate joins their party. Jennifer may have another ten minutes before I welcome her to the party with open arms.

Because in ten minutes time, life should become quite interesting for Jennifer.

Off in a corner of the room, a few feet from the door, is the lightly crisped Kristen. It wasn't challenging to retrieve her body from the kitchen. I simply created another digital facade—in the off-chance Jennifer may walk back in as I dragged her out.

A scream squeals from the monitor and I focus on the screen.

Now she is yelling. Calling out the names of the three other women, as well as Skip and Billie. Laughter bubbles in my chest and rips from my throat.

I relish the exact moment Skip and Billie each took their last breath. Their facial expressions spark the high I crave. And just thinking about them has me soaring through clouds, eager for the next fatality. The ache to feel the high again and again.

And the arousal it delivers.

Every time I have the pleasure of witnessing someone's demise…. How do I explain the elation circulating through my bloodstream in that singular moment? How do I translate the euphoria into words? Being the bearer of their demise…

My heart claws at my ribcage. The wild beast in my soul mauls at my flesh. Tries to escape as my blood heats into a river of magma. As goose flesh prickles my skin and shoots an addictive, electric tingle throughout my body. A light sheen spills from my pores as adrenaline surges to a new plateau.

This type of high… you can't buy this on the streets. The only dealer in this game is yourself. You want the high? Then you must earn it.

Sitting stoic in this secluded room, mere feet from my hand-picked victims, is exhilarating. Although I am not a hands-on killer ninety-five percent of the time, each one of these beauties dies via my hands. Whether it is from a lethally-coated condom, a steel cord at neck level in a never-ending hallway, or a toaster oven with faulty wiring exposed just enough to make things toasty—pun intended.

Their blood is on my hands. And I wouldn't want it any other way.

Pressing a button on the keyboard, the monitor flickers to a different view—the first bedroom in the hall. Kelly, Nina, and Belinda lay peacefully on the bed and sleep soundly. Not one of them has heard a single one of the screams Jennifer has belted out. Not one of them has stirred the slightest.

God bless the art of soundproofing.

But my current interest isn't the three women. My focus is elsewhere. In a dreamlike state of euphoria. A sudden onset of nostalgia fluttering in my chest. With the click of a mouse and a few taps on the keyboard, the camera slowly spins and zooms in on my trophies.

My trophies.

My souvenirs.

The three hundred and seventeen miniature versions of the women—and a handful of men—I have brought here. Who I have played my special games with. And soon, I will add seven more to my collection. Seven new friends to share something singularly special in common with the others—their demise. And me.

I am the common denominator. Me. Only me.

My eyes dance across the screen, My pulse racing as I take in each of my former victims in their new personas. Sally from the hair salon. Listened to everyone's happy stories while she cut and colored and permed their hair. She envied too many. Then, there was Becky from the military resale shop. Always seeking the veteran soldier to love her. Janeen from the strip club. Peeling her clothes off for attention, but never getting enough.

And my all-time favorite... Peter from the accounting firm.

Peter sat in my top three for several reasons. As with most men, he thought he was God's gift to womankind. Thought he was the hottest thing in town. He was hot alright. Hot as a fresh pile of cow shit. He also aided his boss in laundering and embezzling millions of dollars. Peter should have chosen the high ground. Should have told his boss to take a long walk off a short pier.

Instead, he jumped on the bandwagon and decided to live the high life.

Shortly after Peter "went missing", the police frequently visited his workplace. After enough visits, and some digging into Peter's background, the accounting firm was shut down and the CEO received a new pair of bracelets along with a chauffeured ride to federal prison.

Two birds. One very large stone.

That is how Peter died, by the way. A boulder crushing his skull. It was quite a magnificent sight to behold. How easily his brittle skull cracked. His blood oozing out and painting the ground beneath him. Brain matter spattered here and there. Like art.

If I squinted hard enough, I could probably make out the stain.

Snapping out of my stroll down memory lane, I take one last glimpse at my precious keepsakes. "I promise it won't be long. Soon, you'll have new friends. Then, we can sit together, have some tea, and play."

Another click and the monitor flickers back to the living room. Jennifer sits on the edge of the couch, slowly slipping off and plopping down on the floor. Tears stain her cheeks as she trembles head to toe.

Didn't peg her as a crier.

As I do with all my candidates, I followed Jennifer over the last six months. Observed and learned as many of her habits as possible. What she ate. If she drank. Did she smoke? Was she single?

From all of my homework, I discovered she was somewhat of a loner. Not just at home, but also at work. Her job didn't require direct supervision or constant check-ins, so she spent most of her time in the lab alone. Trips to the grocery store—alone. New clothing purchases from the same retailer—alone. Adventures out for dinner, whether she sat in the corner booth or took it home—alone. Even her trips to the movie theater—alone.

Hands down, Jennifer was my easiest target. Ever.

Of all the times I surveilled her, she was never with another person. Sure, she talked on the phone and texted people, but she was always alone. She either enjoyed her solitude or didn't enjoy the obligation of spending time with others. She was a social butterfly, but only on her terms. The parameters always set by her.

No matter. Her life choices made her easy pickings.

Good for me. Not so good for her.

On the floor, she draws her legs to her chest and tucks her head between her chest and knees. She wraps her hands around the front of her legs and rocks gently. Barely discernable, but I see her fingers clench into tight fists. Knuckles whitening under the pressure. Cries weepier. Voice cracking as she continues to call out for help. Again and again.

"No one is coming to save you, my sweet."

It is just you. All alone. As usual. Exactly how you like it.

Her whimpers echo with annoyance in my ears, but

almost softly enough to be inaudible. I count how many times she has sniffled. How many times she has sucked the mucus back in. Over the last ten minutes, she has done it eighteen times.

On the nineteenth drag, her head pops up.

Her eyes widen. All tears and snot vanish. As if they never existed. She paws at her stomach and fumbles forward on her knees, crawling forward a few feet. On all fours, Jennifer takes a deep breath, clamps down on her lips, and shakes her head. The color drains from her face. She turns her face into her shoulder and bites down. Sweat coats her skin as she stares off in the distance with pain in her eyes.

Finally.

Moving slower than a tortoise, she creeps across the floor. Hands and knees wobbly with each trek forward. As she reaches the dining table, she grabs hold of one of the chairs and uses all her strength to hoist herself upright.

Jennifer calls out to no one. Begs for someone to help her. Pleads for anyone to come to her aid. But all she gets is silence. No response. Not a single sound. Except the echo of her own voice bouncing off of the walls.

She clutches the edge of the glass top and moves around the table. When she reaches the side nearest the bathroom, she stops. Her stomach growls in protest and she slaps a hand over her mouth. Reluctantly, she completely lets go of the table and steadies herself before stepping forward.

Once balanced, she hesitantly steps forward. Before taking another step, her face twists in pain. Eyes pinch tightly. Lips bunch and whiten. Her forehead creases as she squeezes her midsection vigorously.

It's about to hit the fan. Literally.

She moves faster now. Stride resembling a zombie with a mission. When she reaches the bathroom doorway, she clings to the frame as the rest of her body lets go.

Her hands slap the tile floor in the bathroom while her knees smack the hardwood in the dining area as she drops on all fours. She claws at the floor, attempting to pull herself toward the toilet. Dragging herself a foot or two in the bathroom, she inches closer to the porcelain bowl.

After her labored trek across the small space, Jennifer clutches the edge of the toilet seat and heaves herself closer. I study every move she makes with eager eyes. My insides vibrate and a wide grin slowly consumes my face as she lifts the seat up and hugs the base of the toilet. She is in a position to vomit.

Which would be her gut reaction. And probably the same for anyone.

But she has no clue what is about to happen. None whatsoever.

She also has no idea the majority of the food in the kitchen is laced with poison. Which rather simple, actually. Lace the foods most likely to be eaten first. Those first foods are simple and quick. And, inevitably, someone would be too impatient to wait for *some*one to make a regular meal. I assumed it would be one of two people.

My first assumption was spot on. "Haven't lost my touch yet."

Jennifer grips the toilet as if her life depends on it. And

then her nose starts to bleed. The hot, red stream drips once. Twice. The droplets blending with the water until no longer visible.

She swipes the back of her hand along her nose and stares at the thick red stripe with wide eyes. Then the blood flows more steadily. Two or three drops per second. The toilet water transitioning from clear to pink to red in a matter of seconds.

Slow sobs leak from her eyes as her body shakes uncontrollably. Wails of pain and fear spill from her lips. Her tears hitting the water alongside the blood from her nose.

Without warning, her hands fly to her stomach and clench the organs beneath the surface. Jennifer stands as quickly as possible and fumbles to unfasten her pants. Once she shoves them down, she sits on the toilet and grabs the small wastebasket between the toilet and tub.

In the same moment she vomits into the wastebasket, her body convulses and forces everything in her intestinal tract out the opposite end.

The visual is retched and grotesque to observe. I only wish I was closer to the action.

Maybe next time.

I tap on the keyboard and the camera zooms in a hair closer. "Guess this is as close to front row as I'm getting."

Her body contracts again and again, working to excrete the poison from every possible outlet. Trying every feasible way to save this human life.

This is the nature of human existence. To expel what our body doesn't need or what is toxic to our well-being. To maintain homeostasis. Maintain our well-oiled machine for as long as possible.

But some toxins cannot be expelled completely. Some toxins get so interwoven in our bloodstream, in our organs, and every cell and atom. With those toxins, there is no way out. Well, actually there is *one* way out. But it is not an option the body or mind desires.

Her body shakes violently and the wastebasket falls to the floor. The contents splatter up and out of the wastebasket, spraying the tile. Jennifer reaches out and grips the pedestal sink, bracing herself as the shaking intensifies.

After a feverish round of tremors, her legs loosen and she topples to the floor. Pants at her knees. Face swimming in a small puddle of her own stomach's contents. She convulses uncontrollably on the floor. Urine and feces exit from one end. White froth foams between her lips as her eyes roll back into her head.

We're almost to the finish line with you, dearest Jennifer.

Her body bucks and thrashes violently for another thirty seconds. Head smacking into the wall over and over and over. Then her movements slow. Her body steadies into one position. And her mouth falls slack, along with her hands and fingers.

I pick up a small doll to my left. Stroke the soft hair with my hand and set it in the chair with the others. A wide smile stretches my cheeks taut as my eyes water with tears of joy.

"And then there were three…"

CHAPTER ELEVEN

KELLY

I CRACK my left eye open and spot the dresser across the room. The daylight has faded away and the room seems almost too dark to see anything with ease. I shift and attempt to roll on my back when I hear a muffled groan behind me on the bed.

Turning my head to the side, I spot Nina and Belinda lying next to me on the king-size mattress. *How long have we been in here?* I bring the palm of my hand to my temple and rub, trying to remember. We came in here after cleaning up the dinner mess in the kitchen. But everything gets a little fuzzy after.

Dinner.

My stomach groans and I slap a hand to my solar plexus, pressing in an attempt to silence it. The groan loud enough to wake a hibernating bear.

God, I'm starving.

Inhaling slow and deep, I roll my eyes closed and relish the delicious aromas permeating the house. Part of me says I should wake Nina and Belinda. Tell them the food must be ready if I smell it throughout the house. But part of me is feeling selfish. As in, I want the food all for myself and as much as possible before anyone else gets their hands or mouths near it.

My stomach growls its agreement and I mentally shush it.

Slowly, I inch off the mattress. My feet then my butt. *Scoot, scoot, scoot.* Like a caterpillar. When I reach the edge, I drop my feet and legs to the floor and rise from the mattress. I peer over my shoulder and don't make out any movement in the dark.

I step forward and the floor creaks as I add weight to a new plank of wood. Pausing, I hiss and glance back at Belinda and Nina again.

Nothing. Neither has budged.

Perfect.

Creeping forward, I inch along at the pace of a sloth. I reach out blindly with my hands and feel for my surroundings. With each step, the room grows darker.

"Just need to find a wall," I whisper into the darkness.

Finally, I hit a wall and trace my hands along the surface until I locate the door and, eventually, the knob. I glance in the direction of where the bed should be, to check on Nina and Belinda, but can no longer see.

Damn, it got dark fast.

I start turning the knob, but hesitate. Then shake off my doubts, turn the knob, and open the door slowly. Creaking breaks the silence—creaking I don't recall when we shut the door.

Light from outside the room penetrates the darkness and temporarily blinds me. When my eyes adjust, I peek over to spot Nina and Belinda still asleep on the bed. I step into the hall and close the door as quietly as possible behind me.

I tiptoe down the hall and into the spacious dining area. As if I have lived here for years, I head for the kitchen and stop before I walk in. But something is different. The energy feels *off*.

The kitchen is walled off and no longer the big, open space. And there is now a door to enter the kitchen. Last I remember, there was no door. Anywhere.

The new superficial view has me walking slower and proceeding with caution. I am tossed up. Should I open the door? One not there thirty-something minutes ago. Or wait for someone to walk out? Normally, I would waltz in without hesitation. But this house—how we all got here— makes me second-guess everything.

"Kristen? Jennifer? You two in there?"

I smell a faint hint of chicken and dumplings and my mouth waters. Another scent floats in the air and I can't quite pinpoint it. Inhaling deeper, I try to place where I have smelled it before. Smoky. A little earthy. Maybe mesquite. Or hickory. Is she cooking barbeque, too?

Damn, I love barbeque ribs.

My mouth waters double time. Impatience takes center stage as my stomach snarls. I push open the door and burst into the kitchen, ready to eat a buffet. No doubt my stomach could handle several platefuls right now.

When I step in, I spot the large pot bubbling on the stove. I heave open the oven door in search of the barbeque, but quickly discover the inside cold and empty.

"Why does it smell like barbeque if there is none?" I ask myself.

I startle when a loud thump cracks behind me as the door swings shut. Which is when I also realize the kitchen no longer looks as it did earlier.

Nowhere near the same. Not remotely close.

In the blink of an eye, the pot of bubbling food on the stove disappeared. Vanished. The scent of my now missing meal still lingers in the air. And my stomach reminds me I haven't eaten in a day or more.

Now, the kitchen is some dark, dilapidated place. I walk back to the entrance and flip the light switch up and down a few times. But nothing happens. The fridge is cracked open and dark inside. I tug the door open further and instantly regret it when a foul odor slaps me in the face. A funk so putrid, I may puke on the spot.

I plug my nose and cover my mouth, but I still smell it. No doubt, it will be locked in my nasal memory for life. The shelves are packed with spoiled packaged food and produce. Some tipped over and leaking. I slam the door shut and back away, reluctant to unplug my nose.

Instead, I head to the cabinets, hopeful I will stumble upon something edible or useful in the dark. Some cabinets have properly hung doors while others are falling off or missing altogether.

I check inside a few of the cabinets and come up empty-handed. The more I search, the more it feels as if my treasure hunt is a lost cause.

Luckily, in the next cabinet, I come across a candle and book of matches. With only two matches left. I tear one of the thin, cardboard sticks from the book and strike the head against the rough patch on the back. The flame glows at the end of my fingertips as I light the candle wick and illuminate the room.

Around me, it appears as if no one has lived here for more than forty or fifty years. In every direction, something is crumbly or barely holding on or coated in filth. I tip my head back and notice the ceiling is bubbled and decayed in the corners. The walls layered with a faded, floral wallpaper which is peeling off at the seams and ends. The cabinets and counters appear hand-crafted from decades ago, but are now being eaten by the elements. And the floor…

I step forward and hear the floor protest beneath me. The plank under my right foot splinters and splits as I move. As gingerly as possible, I head for the exit. Making it to the door without falling through the floor, I swing the door outward and leave.

A whoosh from the door swing extinguishes the candle flame. Instantly, I'm engulfed in utter darkness. A slow creak, followed by a snap rings out. The kitchen door falls from the hinges and bangs against the floor. I shriek and leap out of the way.

Thank God I didn't drop the candle. I dig in my pocket, take the final match in the book, and strike it. *Please don't let me need more.*

With the candlewick glowing once again, I shake the flame out on the match. I hold the candle in front of me and move it side to side. I squint into the darkness in search of anything familiar. It somewhat resembles the dining room from earlier. Except now the room is vacant. A hollow shell.

No table. No chairs.

No pictures on the walls.

No furniture.

Nada.

I head for the hall, in the hopes of returning to Nina and Belinda. Kristen and Jennifer, too. A few steps down the hall, I turn right and walk into the first bedroom. Empty.

No bed.

No dresser.

No Nina, Belinda, Kristen, or Jennifer.

But of all the things to remain in this creepy-ass house, it *would* end up being the hundreds of freaky-looking dolls. And right now, they all seem to be staring at me. Screaming silent pleas. Begging me to run or get help.

Or… I have lost my damn mind.

I back out of the room as quickly as I entered and head for the next bedroom at the end of the hall. The door is cracked open when I approach. I push against the filthy grain and open it fully. As with the first bedroom, this one is also missing all the furniture.

Stepping inside, I spin around and light every corner of the room. The bedroom appears to be just as distressed as the kitchen. As I inch closer to the center of the room, something on the floor catches my eye.

An envelope.

Squatting down, I cup my hand around the flame, and pick up the yellowed envelope. On the front, it says *For Kelly.* Instinctively I scan the room for someone lurking in the dark. But it's no use. I only see a foot or two around me.

I set the candle on the floor and lift the unsealed flap

on the envelope back. A single piece of stationary slides out. I slowly unfold the paper with trembling hands. Frightened and anxious and dying to know what it says.

The note is short. Simple. One hundred percent straight to the point.

Kelly,

You can't spell SLAUGHTER without LAUGHTER.
Four down... three to go.
Soon, my dear, it will be your turn.

D

Four down? What the hell does that mean?

Rooted in place, I read the three lines again and again. And then realization hits me like a baseball bat to the head. My hand flies up to my mouth. If this means what I think it means...

"Skip and Billie and Kristen and Jennifer are." I pause. "They're d-dead," I whisper. "No. It can't be."

I need to get out of here. NOW.

Four down. Skip, Billie, Kristen, and Jennifer are the only four which make sense. I haven't seen them in a while. *Are they the four this D person is referencing?*

Nina and Belinda were okay when I woke up on the bed. But are they now? Everything in the other room, including them, has disappeared. Does this mean they vanished too?

The letter did say *three to go*. I must be one of the three. Nina and Belinda, the other two.

Shit. I need to find them. Warn them something crazy is about to happen. Maybe we can band together.

Maybe we can save each other.

Maybe, together, we can survive.

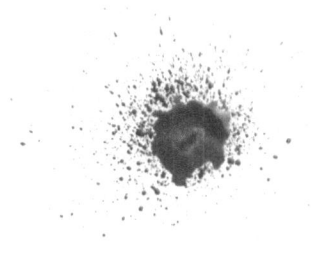

I head for the door, ready to bolt down the hall toward Nina and Belinda. Out in the hall, I slam the door closed behind me and abandon the letter telling me I will die. When I spin around and face the hall, I stumble back.

The hall is no longer a hall.

Now, it is a small room. The size of a tool shed. Maybe seven feet square.

In this new hall, there are only two ways out. Two doors. The one I just exited and one directly across from it. One which previously had multiple, high-tech locks in place. Now...

The door is unwelcome. An eyesore. An absent temptation. But the only other option.

I go to the blank wall on my right and trace the surface in hopes I might discover some hidden exit point. Nothing.

Crossing the small space, I do the same with the opposite wall. Which yields the same result.

I'm aware of what lies behind the door I walked out of —emptiness. Emptiness and a three-line note from the sick fuck behind this whole situation. But who knows? Maybe I will get lucky. Maybe this other door is the actual exit from this hellhole. Which is why it was triple bolted earlier. Because it leads to freedom.

With my newfound optimism, I take a step toward the door and wrap the cool, metal knob with my hand. *Deep breath in, deep breath out. This is the only way.* I twist the knob left and push the door open, but don't move an inch.

Squinting, I peer into the room. But it's so damn dark, I don't see anything. Not even my raised hand. Unsure of what to do next, I freeze. The idea of waltzing into a pitch-black, foreign space freaks me out. Instead, I call out for one of the others.

"Nina? Belinda? You in there? Hello?"

My voice leaks into the darkness and bounces back. Almost an echo, but too perfect in tone and volume. I remain rooted in place while waiting for a response. But no one answers. As eager as I am to learn if this is the way out, the never-ending darkness has me hesitant.

What if it's another dead end? Another empty, dank room. The next nail in the coffin to solidify how trapped I am between this room and the other.

Being confined to these two rooms and the mini hall between them slowly wrenches my heart. My palms sweat as my limbs quake.

Deep breaths, Kelly. You've got this. Deep breaths.

I take a few deep breaths and count to ten before I step forward. *Now or never.* Then take another step. I hold the candle at arm's length and scan the room as much as possible. But it's pointless. The flame does nothing except make me squint to see past it. Basically, I stare at a flame in the middle of a pitch-black room. Step by step, I amble farther into the darkness. I angle the candle left and right in the hopes the light will reveal the shimmer of something in the room.

I inch two steps forward before the door slams shut behind me. My hair brushes against my cheek as a whoosh of air passes and extinguishes the candle flame. Then there is nothing but night. No light from windows or under the door. A strange sense of vacancy and hollowness consumes me. I may have lost my sight, but it suddenly seems as if I see all the things no one should.

Like staring into the void.

"Hello?" I whisper into the room.

The singular word bounces back at me, distorted by some machine. The eerie, mechanical hello repeats over and over. And I lose count of how many times I've heard my own voice be manipulated. Sometimes, the voice is sweet and childlike. Other times, it's deep and venomous. So bone-chilling, I wrap my arms around my midsection and attempt to protect myself from whoever else is in this room.

The different variations echo less than a second after the previous. On my left. On my right. Above me. Below. In my face. Against my ear from behind.

Something brushes against my arm and a chill slithers up my spine. *Someone is in here.* I make myself smaller, crouching down on the floor and bringing my legs to my chest. Something whooshes on my left and, instinctually, I scoot to my right.

A wretched smell invades my nasal cavities and bile rises in my throat. *What is that?* The room reeks of overfull portable toilets. I suck in a deep breath and attempt to hold it, but the foul odor dominates my senses. Arms wrap around me and I jump, exhaling in fear. I kick and scream, but the person behind me doesn't budge. They just hold me in place and wait for me to stop.

Once I settle, the person tightens one arm and releases the other. Then, a cloth is slapped over my nose and mouth and pressed firmly against my face.

I wriggle and scream into the cloth, but it's no use. Whoever this is, they are much stronger than me. I fight as long as possible, but soon my eyes grow heavy as my mind fogs over and my limbs turn to rubber.

As my eyes drift shut, an overhead light flickers on. In the corner, something catches my eye. Four bodies. Piled on top of each other like garbage. But as quick as I spot them, the world goes black again.

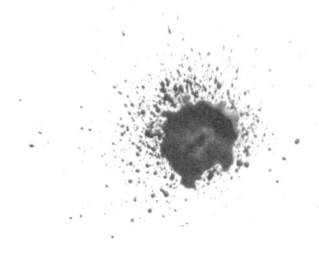

Blinding white light consumes my vision. Too bright

doesn't remotely define the light.

I squint to protect my eyes and try to scan the room between my lashes. But it's no use. My eyelids ache from the constant strain. I slowly peel my lids open. Soon, the light shifts from high beams in my face to stadium lighting. Bright, but bearable.

I examine the new space with fresh eyes. But it's not long before confusion creeps in and settles low in my gut.

The room is spacious. Maybe a two-car garage converted into an interior room. Solid concrete, windowless walls. Splatter stains here and there. And the foul stench of piss and shit lingers in the air. As if an animal has repeatedly gone on the rug for years and no one cares.

As I visually trail around the room, I stop when I reach the opposite corner.

Is that a pile of... *Holy shit!*

Just before I blacked out, I remember seeing four bodies lying in a pile. I crane my neck, narrow my eyes, and focus on the bodies in front of me.

A hairy, masculine arm sticks out at the base.

Skip.

Next, I spy a head of blonde hair laying beside the pile... not attached to a body. I easily make out the features.

Billie.

Then, a charred female lays one body below the top. A silver charm bracelet dangles from her wrist. I search my memory bank and recall seeing a similar bracelet while we made dinner in the kitchen.

Kristen.

Lastly, at the top of the pile is a dark brunette with pants around her ankles. Just a slight view of her profile is visible. Blood paints every speck of her face while vomit coats her hair.

Jennifer.

Oh… My… God… Is this place some sort of tomb?

I wiggle in place, trying to stand and inch closer to the door. But I can't. I'm pinned in place.

Looking down, I see the glint of the metal shackled around my ankles. At my sides, my wrists are cuffed also. Both pairs connected to chains which link to the wall behind me.

How did I not feel the weight of them before?

Perhaps fear overrode every sense except my vision until reality sunk in. But now that I'm aware, it's time to get out of here.

I lift my arms, flick my wrists, and wrap the chains around my forearms. Clutching at the cold metal, I yank away from the wall and try to free myself from the restraints.

But nothing happens. Not a single change. Not even a minor crack in the wall.

I give it another go and it yields the same result.

After several failed attempts, the light in the room dims. A creaking sound pierces the air and sends chills up my spine the same as nails on a chalkboard. The door opens wide enough for someone to enter and someone steps in.

Small in stature, the person is of similar height and build to me. Petite. As in a woman kind of petite.

Dressed in all black, her clothes hang loose on her frame. Decked out in a hoodie with the hood up to blanket her hair. Face disguised with a piece of fabric and a mask with small holes for her eyes, nose, and mouth. Hands protected by gloves. Not a single part of her flesh is visible, except near the holes in the mask.

She stalks toward me. The way she moves… it is both graceful and robotic. Her small frame is lithe and intimidating beneath the bagging attire.

A foot in front of me, she pauses and tilts her head to the side and silently watches me. The creep factor goes from one to ten in a heartbeat. Instinctually, I push back into the cold concrete in an attempt to add more space between us. But my efforts are useless since I'm chained to the goddamn wall.

The only way I will be able to leave these chains is if she allows it. And, by the looks of it, the only way I will leave these chains is if I no longer breathe.

As if reading my thoughts, her head straightens—eyes glued to mine—and tilts the other direction. Studying me. And I can't tell if she is toying with me or reading my mind. Either way, my gut instinct screams to escape. To find an exit and run.

I open my mouth, ready to bargain for my life, but she holds up a hand and stops me.

Is it so wrong for me to plea for my life? To strike a deal with this stranger. To see if she will make an exception for me. Although I don't know her, it is worth a shot.

I have no clue where I am. No one here was familiar. If she were to let me go, I would vow to forget any of this ever happened. And I wouldn't tell a soul. No one would believe me anyway.

Eager to offer my proposal, I open my mouth again. "I'd like to make—"

Her hand flies up again and signals me to stop. To shut my mouth. At this point, what do I have to lose?

"…an offer. I won't—"

She shoves her hand in my face. The sheer force of it makes me close my eyes briefly as my head jerks back.

"I won't say anything to—"

Her hand retreats. She lowers all digits but one and waggles it. Then, she clucks her tongue at me as if disappointed. She takes one step back. Then another. And another. But her eyes never veer away from mine. When she reaches the other side of the room, I drop my gaze and, for the first time, notice a small table littered with objects I can't make out from here.

A hand hovers above said objects as she contemplates which one to pick up. After a couple passes, her hand finally stops. I still cannot see her face, but instinct tells me a wicked glean rests on it. She lowers her hand and wraps her fingers around the object she desires.

When she spins to face me again, my stomach drops to the floor and terror blasts into my bloodstream. In her hand, held high like a prize, is a rather large hunting knife. The blade near a foot long and painted with a dry layer of red. *Is that someone else's blood?* Someone who didn't come here with me and the other six?

Bile rises in my throat and the urge to puke is powerful.

She stalks across the room, regarding me like a doe in the lion's den. Lessening the space between us in a small zig-zag pattern. Head tipping left to right and back again as she closes in on me.

Mere inches away, she slips a hand in her pocket. She retrieves a small remote and waves it at me. The small gadget is decked out with several buttons. I lock on to her every movement before her thumb rests on one. The shackles and chains at my ankles and wrists jingle as my body rattles with nervousness. I fear what happens next.

Before my mind wanders at the possibilities, she presses the button… and vanishes.

Matter-of-fact, every single thing in the room vanishes. Her. The bodies. The table. And my restraints.

I bolt for the door. But as soon as I take a step forward, all light in the room disappears.

I reach forward, knowing the door is only steps away. As soon as I feel the grain beneath my palm, I sigh in relief.

I am getting out of here. Thank god!

Just as I grab hold of the doorknob, a sharpness pierces my right side. The burn is hellacious and like nothing I have ever experienced before. And then I feel another jab— this time on my left. My hand drops from the door and reaches for the pain source. When I land on it, I discover wet heat.

Am I bleeding? Fuck!

And then it happens again, over the back of my right lung.

The light flips on again—brighter than before—and I stare down at my hand. My palm is nothing but a sea of red. I stumble back a step and gasp. With a couple feet between me and the door, I see her better now.

She stands close to me, hand above her head, wielding the knife. She cocks her head and the mask plumps where I imagine her cheeks would be. Stepping closer to me, she lurches forward and strikes me. The knife penetrates my breast and slides in like warm butter.

I falter back and reach for my chest. She lunges forward and brings the knife to the opposite side of my chest. This time when I stumble back, I smack the wall and slide down until my butt meets the floor.

I curl in a fetal position as best I can and try to protect myself. When I don't hear or feel anything for fifteen labored breaths, I peek around the room to see where she is.

Magically, she has disappeared. Again. My breathing kicks into high gear and my heart pounds voraciously in my chest.

Before I have a chance to fold back in on myself, she shows herself again and jabs the knife in my chest near my sternum. Once. Twice. Three times. I squeal into the silence. All I hear now is my frantic heart. The chambers vigorously pumping as the organ focuses on keeping me alive. The harder it works, the more blood spills from my body.

Soon, my pulse slows. Blood pools around me. My breathing shallows.

She squats down in front of me. "Hate to be the bearer of bad news, but you were never getting out of here, little Kelly." Then she lifts the mask. Allows me to take all of her in. And shows me the last thing I will see before my heart stops beating.

Her.

CHAPTER TWELVE

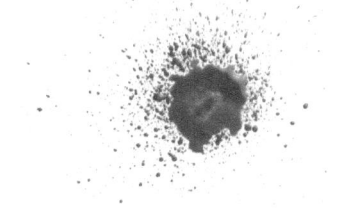

BELINDA BOLTED off the mattress as a scream ricocheted through the air. Her pulse pounded viciously as a light sheen of sweat blanketed her skin. She scanned the dark room with narrowed eyes while her hands patted along the bed until she reached the bedside table.

Her fingers skirted over the table in search of the lamp she remembered seeing earlier. As she traced the surface, a layer of dust caked under her fingers. Finally, she located the lamp base. Cool metal with a round, intricate pattern at the base and smooth metal for the post. Belinda trailed the thin post in search of a twist-knob or chain. Near the bulb, the back of her hand brushed against a chain. She tugged on the end, squinted into the now brightened room, and noticed Nina still asleep on the bed.

But Kelly was gone.

With a hand on Nina's shoulder, Belinda lightly jostled her. "Nina. Nina. You need to wake up."

Nina grumbled softly, rolled on her side and faced away from Belinda. Belinda jostled Nina again and pleaded quietly with her to wake. Nina grumbled louder and swatted behind her in an attempt to wave off whoever disturbed her.

"Nina, get up," Belinda said louder and with more authority.

Slowly, Nina opened her eyes and peered over her shoulder at Belinda. "Ugh… what's the matter?" Her voice thick with sleep.

"Sorry to wake you. Kelly isn't in here anymore and I swear I heard someone scream a moment ago."

Nina sat up and looked around the room, brows scrunched together. Hands at her face, she rubbed the sleep from her eyes.

Belinda walked around the bed and went to the door. She stood waiting for Nina, tapping her nails on her crossed arms while keeping her impatient thoughts to herself. Nina gave an apologetic smile and scurried off the bed a little quicker.

Nina sidled up beside Belinda just as she opened the door and stepped into the hall.

"Kelly?" Belinda called out. "You okay?"

The house laid silent. Eerily silent.

Belinda stepped farther from the bedroom and headed for the dining room. She called out again; this time for anyone. "Jennifer? Kristen? You there?"

But no one responded. She spun around to see Nina on her heels, shoulders bunched and mouth pinched to one side. Belinda signaled for them to go toward the kitchen and Nina nodded.

Walking in stride, the two women inched across the bare dining room and stopped in front of the kitchen door. Nina tapped Belinda on the shoulder. "Do you remember there being a door? I don't even remember there being a wall." She pointed to where the kitchen was once exposed to the dining room.

"This house is fucking crazy. Earlier, when we were all in the living room, the entire house changed in the blink of an eye. At this point, I'm beginning to wonder if we're even in a house."

Nina nodded. The house did keep shifting and changing. As if a chameleon hiding in plain sight.

Belinda pushed the kitchen door open and immediately shielded her eyes as bright light smacked her in the face. "Kristen? Jennifer? You guys in here?" Belinda stepped in with Nina glued to her back.

Just as the door whooshed behind them, the room morphed. The entry still resembled the previous kitchen, but with each passing second, inch-by-inch, the kitchen transformed into the end of the hallway. A few steps forward, Belinda and Nina stood at the end of the hall and the kitchen disappeared.

Belinda glanced over her shoulder and spotted Nina still with her. "What the hell just happened? How are we in the hallway? Feel like I'm losing my goddamn mind. Could've sworn we were in the kitchen five seconds ago."

Nina nodded. "We were in the kitchen. Don't know how, but the kitchen turned into the hallway and then it just... how is this even possible?"

"No idea, but let's see if we can find anyone and ask if they know."

They walked down the hall, back into the dining room and headed for the living room.

"Hello? Anyone here?"

Belinda reached out and skimmed one of the living room walls. She landed on a light switch and flipped it up. When the light flickered on, an empty, pristine living room filled their vision.

They walked in and sat on the couch and dropped their heads in their hands. Nina mumbled against her palms. "I don't understand. Where *is* everyone?"

"Wish I knew."

As Nina sat up, she audibly gasped and Belinda immediately lifted her head. Both women sat motionless with dropped jaws.

A wall lined with shelves appeared out of thin air. Evenly spread out, hundreds of porcelain dolls stared back at them. Confusion marred their features as they looked around the room and noticed they were no longer on the couch in the living room, but on the same bed they slept in less than thirty minutes ago.

"What in the *hell* is going on?" Belinda bellowed out.

"I think someone's trying to mess with our heads. Maybe we should stay put until we figure out where to go from here."

"Figure out what?" Belinda barked out. "Don't mean to be rude, but whoever is screwing with us isn't simply going to stop because we stay in one place."

Nina shrugged. "Well, I don't have any better ideas. We can't seem to find anyone. The house keeps changing where we are. And I'm not sure there's much else we can do."

Belinda dropped her shoulders and hung her head as she whispered, "There has to be something…"

The two women sat idle as they went through various scenarios in their heads. Neither lacked intelligence, but their smarts laid in specific fields.

After a while, Nina broke the silence. "Maybe we should keep trying to go into different rooms. Maybe, eventually, we'll end up in the right room. We can't simply give up after two tries."

Belinda studied Nina a moment. "Guess you're right. I mean, what else are we going to do? If we just sit here, we'll end up dying."

In agreement to try every possible option, the two women got up and headed for the door. When they stepped into the hall, Nina suggested they check the back bedroom first.

They strode down the hall, entered the back bedroom, and waited for the room to change.

At first, it remained the same—large bed, sparse furniture, devoid of light. They took two steps forward—side by side—and called out for the others as their eyes scanned the room. As Belinda opened the closet door, the room brightened and morphed into the kitchen. The same kitchen they were in when they helped Kristen make dinner.

Belinda turned to look for Nina and spotted her at the opposite end of the room. "Think I might be sick," Belinda announced as she clutched her stomach. With one hand on her belly, Belinda grasped the counter as her eyes pinched tightly.

Nina strode across the room and rubbed up and down

her back in a motherly manner to soothe her. "Just take some deep breaths. Keep your eyes closed and try to adjust. Tell your body someone is playing a game with your mind."

Belinda hung her head and nodded. She stood still a moment; palms flattened on the cool granite as she inhaled slow, full breaths into her lungs. After several deep breaths, Belinda opened her eyes and lifted her head.

"Better?"

"Yes. Obviously, my head can't handle this. Good thing video games and virtual reality aren't my thing."

At Belinda's declaration, they stopped breathing and stared at one another. Each of their eyes held the same question. Both of their faces bore the same awe.

Did they just figure out part of the puzzle? Did they find a major clue in this messed-up game?

They continued to stare at one another as if the biggest answer was just laid in front of them—as a joke, no less.

Nina broke their introspection first. "Do you think that's what is happening to us? That we're in some kind of game? Are we in some false reality?"

Belinda let the thought roll around in her head—eyes glazing over as she wondered about the possibility. "I don't know. But how else do we explain what's happening? Earlier, the living room changed from filthy to immaculate in a blink. The same with the rest of the house. Now, every time we walk into a room, it changes into another room. As if someone is deliberately keeping us where they want us." She huffs out a breath. "And where is everyone else?"

This question stirred a new series of questions neither of them had answers to.

Did the others leave? Did they leave and forget Belinda and Nina were still here? Why would someone let the others leave, but hold the two of them captive? Why did the rooms keep changing? What was the point behind all of it? Why?

She let go of the counter and tested her ability to stand without the extra support. After standing steadily for five breaths, Belinda walked to the fridge and opened the door. Scanning the contents, she grabbed a bottled water and closed the door.

Cracking the lid, Belinda took a long pull from the bottle then offered it to Nina. Nina shook her head and darted around the kitchen, opening cabinets and drawers.

"What are you looking for?"

"Food, for starters. I don't know about you, but I'm starving. And maybe some sort of clue as to what is going on."

She continued searching the kitchen and smiled when she discovered a lone box of saltine crackers. She tore open the thin paperboard box and yanked out a sleeve of crackers. She tugged at the plastic until one end burst open and crackers spilled out.

Handing Belinda a sleeve of crackers, Nina said, "You better hold on to these. Who knows how much longer we'll be in here. Or if we'll find food again."

Belinda nodded, took the crackers and opened them with a little more finesse than Nina. After chomping on a couple crackers, they agreed to move on and search for the others in a different room.

Nina held on to the saltines for dear life and told Belinda she was ready. They sidled up next to each other, exited the kitchen, and stepped into the dining area… waiting for it to take them to the next place.

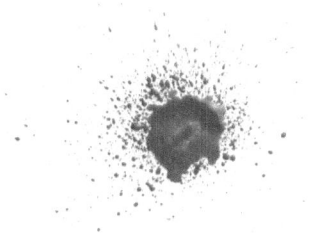

NINA

We walk out of the kitchen, me armed with most of the crackers and Belinda hanging on to her own sleeve and a bottle of water. We get about five feet into the dining room, almost to the table, when the air crackles. The same crackle you hear near power lines. When you stand too close and you literally hear the energy—the raw power—coursing through the lines.

It is about to happen again. We are about to be transported from the dining room to someplace else.

But where?

"It's happening again. I hear it. Maybe close your eyes and brace yourself."

With the last shift, Belinda didn't do so well. For a moment, I thought maybe I'd lose her. Her skin rapidly paled before she braced herself against the counter. Prior to being here, I witnessed people black out. And Belinda displayed several signs.

She shifted her water bottle into the same hand as the crackers and placed her free hand on the table. Pinching her eyes tightly, she bows her head and firmly grips the table. As she drops her head, the room transforms.

The dining table shrinks as does the room around us. Seconds later, we are teleported to a different room. I squint at the light change and wait for my eyes to adjust. As my vision regulates, I decipher where we are now.

I softly tap Belinda on the shoulder. "I think it's over now. Take your time opening your eyes."

She nods beside me with her head hung low. After several deep breaths, she raises her head to slowly take in the room. The foyer. She lets go of the small table beside the front door and tests her balance.

"How are you feeling?" I have genuine concern for how her body is handling everything. Because it might also happen to me.

"Better than last time. Thank goodness." Relief floods her voice as a smile tugs up the corners of her mouth.

We stand stock-still a moment, study every inch of the small foyer and come to the conclusion it all appears the same. Everything except one thing.

The front door.

Last time everyone crowded around the front door, Skip attempted to break the three high-tech locks on the door. Three locks which were no longer there. Now, the door resembled your typical front door. Heavy. Wood. Painted white.

I tap Belinda on the shoulder and point to the door. "The locks are gone."

A new flurry of hope and excitement has us both smiling. The prospect of leaving is less of an illusion. For a moment, the concept feels unreal—another facade in this house of mirrors. We glance at each other, then the door.

After several hours. After the unending craziness which brought the seven of us together. And after the endless number of mind games thrown our way, one thought crossed my mind.

Was it all a test?

A test to see if we could handle the madness. A test to see what we were made of or how resilient we are. Or perhaps a test of time. Of patience. Is that all this was? Nothing but a test. Someone's sick experiment.

The bigger question, though, is this our reward for passing? The opportunity to leave. Nothing to hold us back. Nothing to keep us captive. Freedom.

Taking a few steps forward, I put the front door in arm's reach. Belinda and I stare at each other. Neither of us certain of who should turn the knob. Who should grant us our freedom?

I reach out, slide my fingers around the cool metal and twist to the right. The handle turns and a surge of joy erupts in my belly. I yank the handle and the door catches.

Belinda blinks over at me and shrugs. "Maybe there's a lock on the handle."

Letting the knob go, we both lean in to get a better view. I inspect the left while Belinda scans the right. When we're done, both of us shake our heads and frown.

"Maybe it was just stuck. Try it again. Surely, this door doesn't get used much."

I grab the knob again, twist and yank. It doesn't budge. So, I give it a firmer tug. It moves a fraction, so I repeat the process and it loosens a little more. Again and again. My hope inflates with each new movement of the door. Soon, the door will open and we will leave this place. I yank on the door one last time and the door flies open.

Freedom.

I stare past the open door in awe. In front of us is a small wooden porch with steps leading down to a narrow path with trees lining either side. Belinda and I gape at each other, then back out the door with our mouths hanging open.

Can't believe this is happening. After everything we have dealt with in this house, I can't believe this moment is real.

I look over at Belinda. "You ready to get the hell out of here?"

"Hell yes I am."

We are about to step out the door. About to walk away and take a huge, fulfilling breath of freedom when something catches my attention. A faint sound. At first, I wonder if my mind is playing tricks on me. Until I hear it again.

I extend my arm out to the side and block Belinda from exiting. "Did you hear that?"

"Hear what?"

I press a finger to my lips and lean in the direction I heard the sound. Then I hear it again. Sounds like a woman, calling out in the distance.

"Did you hear it that time?"

"I didn't hear anything. What on earth are you talking about?"

I hear it again. This time it's loud enough to discern it is a woman's voice—maybe Jennifer—calling out for help. A second later, I hear it again.

"Jennifer? Is that you? Can you hear me?" I belt out.

Belinda cocks her head as her brows squish together and she grimaces. "I don't hear anything. What the hell are you hearing?"

"I swear Jennifer keeps calling out for help," the call cries again. "Tell me you didn't just hear that. Just now."

"Didn't hear anything. I think whoever has been messing with us is messing with only you right now."

I don't understand. How the hell can I hear something, but she cannot? Perhaps someone is messing with my head, but how can they make it so only I hear it? With all the craziness which has happened since we arrived, whenever something happened, we all noticed. At least those of us together. How is it possible for it to be any different now?

I hear her cries again. *Help me!* Her scream sounds as if it's down the hallway. Maybe from the bedroom. Each time I hear the SOS, it gets louder. Each time I hear it, the more desperate and afraid she sounds.

As badly as I want to bolt out this door right now, I also want to save her. It wouldn't feel right if I deserted someone I could have saved.

Louder and louder. As if she stands beside me and screams in my ear. I gaze at Belinda and she simply stares back with a bunched forehead. My eyes bounce back and forth between the interior of the house and the world beyond the front door. Torn by what to do. Should I follow my morality and find Jennifer? Or should I abandon my sense of judgment and leave?

This may be the only opportunity to escape.

But if I walk out the door—if I leave someone behind I could have saved—I will never forgive myself. Knowing I didn't at least try to save another person's life will eat at me for as long as I live. I can't handle guilt of that magnitude.

I face the inside of the house as the cry for help belts out again. As I take a step, Belinda grabs my bicep and halts me in place.

"Where are you going?" She points outside. To freedom. To our shot at escaping. "This is the way out."

Gah, I don't know what to do. As desperately as I want to leave this insane asylum, I also want to save the woman who steadily cries out with sweet desperation. I want to save her because I believe in karma. If it were me screaming, I would hope like hell someone would hear me. And hopefully that someone would come and help me.

"I know, but... I realize you can't hear her cries, but I can. And if I abandon her and could've saved her... how am I supposed to live with guilt like that?"

All I hope is that she gets where I'm coming from. How I am not asking her to stick by my side while I find this person. Maybe she should leave and go find help for all of us. The idea swims laps in my head and I think it is the best option we have.

"Belinda, go. Leave here. Go find help. I'll go find Jennifer, if that is who it is, and help her. While I do that, you run out the front and find someone, anyone, to help us all."

Belinda stares at me, frozen in place, and unsure what to do next. I practically see the waging war in her eyes. Her mind spitting out rapid-fire choices, but unable to choose which of them she should give in to. She looks out the front door, then back into the house where she claims she can't hear the screams. Her eyes meet mine as she shakes her head. "I can't leave you here, alone. If something happens to you, and I'm not here to try and help... I'll never be able to forgive myself."

She hangs her head and slumps. The letdown of not leaving now is obvious. I don't want her to feel obligated. Don't want her to feel like if she leaves, something bad will happen to me and whoever screams. "Believe me, I get it, but someone needs to save all of us. The opportunity is right in front of us. In front of me. Maybe there's a reason only I can hear the screams. Maybe I'm meant to help whoever it is, while you're meant to help us all. Belinda, it's okay. I'll be okay."

She simply stares at me as the war still riots inside her head. "No. I may not be able to hear whatever you're hearing, but I have a strong feeling we need to stick together."

She reaches for the door, pulls on the handle and closes it. An eerie silence takes over the space around us as we stand there and figure out our next move.

Another cry reverberates off the walls, louder now with the door closed. I glance at Belinda, tap a finger to my ear, and non-verbally ask her if she heard anything. Her eyes drop down and she shakes her head, devastation written in her posture.

Placing a hand on her shoulder, I give it a gentle squeeze. "It's okay. Just follow my lead." She nods and we walk back into the house.

As we step into the dining room, the cry echoes again, and I point toward the hallway. We walk in slow, measured steps and make as little noise as possible.

We walk past the bathroom—empty. Past the first bedroom—empty. The cry calls out again—the scream pierces the air and elicits a chill throughout my body. Walking up to the second bedroom—empty. I spin around in the hall to the one and only door which remains. The door as securely bolted as the front once was. Now it only has a knob and a deadbolt.

As I reach for the door, one notion passes through my head. An idea which jolts me.

Why hasn't the house played tricks on us since we abandoned the front door?

CHAPTER THIRTEEN

CAPTOR

INTRIGUING.

After playing mind games with the final two for—I check my watch—the last hour, shock and disbelief and pleasure infiltrate me. I lean back in my black and burgundy throne, utterly fascinated. Observing them as they ponder whether they should walk out the front door or stay here and help a complete stranger.

Scenarios such as these always captivate me. How the brain works. How it chooses to do one thing and abandon another. When it opts for destruction over peace, more times than not. Believe me, I have witnessed several choose another's life over their own. Most of the saviors? They're women. As if the desire to help is embedded in their DNA.

Nina and Belinda stand at the door, stare past the porch to the path dividing the trees. Trees which block the house from street view and neighbors. A street not so far from where they stand.

The house is hidden, though. The sounds of what happens beyond the wooded acreage muffled from wandering ears. Trees, shrubs, and a plethora of plant life…

all of it hindering the whizz of passing cars and the occasional dog barking.

I press a button on the remote in my palm and smile as the desperate plea of Jennifer crying out for help breaks the airwaves. Awaiting what happens next, I gasp as Nina lifts her head, but Belinda doesn't. Hmmm. Quite interesting.

I couldn't be certain it would actually work, but it seems I have set the perfect frequency for one of them. I'd messed with the wavelengths, time and again, with the last menagerie and had it almost perfect.

But now, as I watch the two women stand there. The final two with beating hearts and ability to breathe—unbeknownst to them. A shiver of pleasure ripples in my veins as I study them closely. As one hears the cries of a dead woman while the other stares at her like she has lost her goddamn mind.

Fucking priceless.

My heart beats its fists against my ribcage. Sweat breaks out across my skin. Heat skyrockets from the crown of my head to the tips of my toes. I press the plus sign for the volume once, then the play button and relish in delight as only one of them hears the futile cry. When Nina leans toward the sound, intense need tugs low in my core.

Fuck! Can't wait for them all to die at my hands.

I reach between my legs and press on the aching need growing heavier with each passing second. The yearning screams—always hungry for more—and brings me back to my first kill. Who doesn't find satisfaction in their first? The one who popped the proverbial cherry. Mine was a bombshell—and a complete accident—which turned into the most incredible high ever experienced.

Mandy Peterson.

We'd been messing around for weeks. Sweet kisses turning hungry. Hand-holding turning into hands roaming. God, she was beautiful.

After playing this game of cat and mouse a few weeks, things grew hotter and more intense. Can't speak for her, but I was constantly horny and just kissing and feeling her tits wasn't doing it for me anymore.

I told her I wanted more—to at least slip my fingers inside her—and she agreed without resistance.

There we were, two teenagers rolling around on the bed. Hands between the other's legs. Grunts and groans of pleasure floating in the air.

At some point, I took the lead. My fingers pulsed in and out of her wet walls while I wrapped my other hand around her throat. Every time I squeezed a little harder, it seemed to turn both of us on more.

I got so wrapped up in the sensation of her impending orgasm, I paid no mind to how hard I was squeezing her trachea. When her orgasm exploded around my fingers, I tightened my grip around her throat and delighted in the pool of moisture between my own legs.

By the time I reined in my own bliss, I peeked up and saw her lifeless body under my hand.

At first, I freaked out. But the more I stared down at her, the more my insides tightened, the more my core flooded with desire.

The sight of her limp body skyrocketed my arousal. Turned me on like nothing else.

Staring at her dead body a moment, I warred with what to do next. Before I gave attention to my next move, I had my hands between my legs. Satiating the beast—the heightened hunger—inside me. When my body detonated in a vicious explosion incomparable to any prior, I was hooked. Wanted more. Would never get enough.

And now... watching each and every one of these people perish. An inferno brews deep inside me. White hot flames lick every inch of my skin. My molten hot blood pooling at the apex of my thighs. Each cry for help just adds fuel to the blaze. I press play again and grin wickedly as Nina stares back into the house, unable to leave someone behind. It stirs a primal urge in my core and I slip my hand between my legs and rub.

I bump up the volume another notch and press play in ten-second intervals. With my hand wedged between my thighs, I stare at the screen as they discuss Belinda leaving to find help versus Belinda's desire to not leave Nina alone. They debate for a moment and rattle off the potential outcome of both scenarios. I'm dying to know which avenue Belinda will take, but I have a feeling I already know the answer.

A moment later, Belinda rewards with the decision I assumed she would make all along.

One rule of thumb I learned over the years... know your victims. Almost every person I hand-selected is—was—selfless. But each time I go through the process of choosing them, I know at least one must be selfish. A know-it-all. An I-can-get-us-out-of-here type.

On the monitor, I chuckle as the front door closes and the two women walk back into the house in search of Jennifer. Seeing as Nina is the only one who can hear the repetitive recording, Belinda is completely blind to what is really happening.

Jennifer's mechanically played cry calls out again and Nina makes a hand signal for Belinda to head toward the hallway. Nina pushes open the bathroom door and they look inside. I snicker at the reminiscence of where Jennifer took her last breath. They step farther into the hall and head for the first bedroom, staying close to the door.

They search the parts of the room they can see, not spotting Jennifer. While they loiter, I zoom in on the wall which holds my trophies. My most prized possessions. My pets. I could tell you how each and every one of the people those dolls represents died. Just thinking about each of them triggers a delicious shiver across my skin and fever between my legs.

Nina and Belinda seem as if they're ready to search elsewhere, so I entice them further and press the button. Nina hops into action and heads for the next bedroom, on a mission to find the woman behind the cries.

Darting down the hall, they search the second bedroom from the doorway and find the space to be exactly the same. Empty. I press the button again and watch as Nina whips her head around and stares at the only other door in the hall. The door none of them have entered.

Nina strides across the hall and stands in front of the ominous door. She watches it a moment as she angles her head to the side. Nina leans in, presses her ear to the door and listens. Counting to thirty, she stands motionless in the quiet. Teasing and tormenting is my version of foreplay, and I am loving every second.

Then I press the button again, the scream for help echoes in the room around me and passes through the door to her.

Belinda steps closer to Nina and asks what is happening. "Heard her again. I think she's in here." Nina points to the door. "It looks different now. Only one lock. Maybe we can kick it in or something."

To goad her further... *play*. The sweet, delicious and desperate cry calls out once more and Nina loses it.

Her hands beat on the door as she calls out to Jennifer. Asks Jennifer if she can hear her voice. Tells her they are going to help. *Bam! Bam! Bam!* Nina beats against the door again as her attempts to soothe a dead woman continue.

All the while...

I rise from my plush throne and monitors and walk to the wall behind me. Over to the two large cages. The cages I eagerly wait to lift the gates on. I traipse my fingertips along the frigid cold metal and a shiver of excitement pulses in my veins.

Squeezing a hand between the bars of one cage, then the next, I nestle my fingers in the fur of my two most sacred friends. The bitches who will protect me to no end. Two comrades who will never let me down. Who will never abandon me. And who will obey any and every command I give them.

Pressing a button on top of each cage, both doors slowly rise. My two faithful friends sit in their confines and await my command.

I hold up my palm with three fingers upright and together. They amble out of the cages and go sit beside the door. When I reach them, they look up at me and watch as I bring the flatter side of my fist to my lips before spreading the digits.

On cue, both dogs change their stance. Position themselves for a fight. Hackles raised, teeth bared, growls filtrating through the banging on the other side. They are locked and loaded and ready. Ready to do one thing and one thing only.

Defend and protect.

And in the only manner I have shown them. To the death.

I reach for the bolt on the door and prepare to release my beauties. I lean down with my mouth between their ears. "Go bring me my prize."

And I unleash them upon the last two of the unknowing.

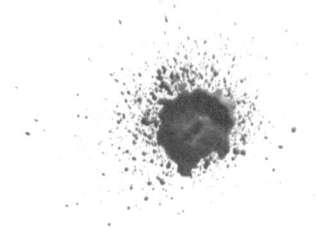

BELINDA

Something is far beyond wrong in this whole scenario. If someone was trapped on the other side of this door, screaming for her life, wouldn't I hear her too? Nothing is normal about screams bellowing out of a house and only one person hearing the cries. It doesn't matter what kind of supersonic hearing you have, it simply isn't *normal*.

Nina bangs relentlessly on the door. Jiggling the handle left and right. Rattling it back and forth as she beats her fist with abandon. Her voice grows more and more raspy as she yells for Jennifer. Minutes pass and the only noise echoing around us is Nina's clenched fist and hoarse cries. No matter how hard she tries, the door won't budge.

And I have yet to hear a damn thing.

A chill spreads throughout my body and seeps deep in my bones. Nothing good can come of this scenario. My intuition berates me for not running out the door when the opportunity presented itself.

Everything regarding this house is odd. Mysterious. Frightening. From the structure to all the people who were brought here.

We have been here less than twenty-four hours, yet it feels as if a week has passed. So much has happened in such a short period of time.

Since our arrival, the house has changed appearances three times. Everyone except me and Nina has magically vanished into thin air. The house shifted us from one room to another without effort. And before being placed where we are now, someone has fucked with our heads for who knows how long.

How is this any different? How is it Nina doesn't comprehend the idea this is all a game? A sick and twisted fucking game. Nina bangs on the door because she hears screams. Screams only heard by her. Why can't she grasp how incomprehensible this is?

There is a reason I cannot hear them.

A reason she is the focus.

Whoever is fucking with us doesn't want me to hear it.

Wants Nina drawn to a specific place in the house.

A twinge bursts in the pit of my stomach. Something more is happening here. Something nowhere near right. Why has it taken me so long to figure this out? Obviously, this whole situation would end badly. Intuition told me as much. But why did I choose to ignore everything happening in front of my eyes?

A noise disrupts my introspection. A deep growl. The snarl quiet and low. Wondering if she can hear it too, I tap Nina on the shoulder to get her attention. She stops beating on the door and drops her hand from the knob as she turns to face me. I mouth *stop for a second* and tap a finger to my ear. She tilts her head as questions flit through her eyes.

She drops her hand and we don't breathe as we silently listen for noise on the other side of the door. A soft, menacing growl vibrates the door, followed by deep, rapid inhalations near the floor-door gap. We lock eyes with each other as Nina's mouth slackens and her eyes widen. Surely, I give her the exact same expression.

Dog.

At the same time, we step away from the door. Walking backward with our eyes zeroed in on the door and wondering how a dog is suddenly inside the house. Louder than before, a growl escapes the four-legged monster on the other side. Paws and nails scrape the floorboards and door. When a second snarl joins the mix, we both jump back startled, and back away quicker.

Nausea is a ticking timebomb in my stomach. Any second, I will vomit.

Why didn't we leave when we had the opportunity? Why did I stay when my intuition screamed at me to get the hell out? We should have bolted out the door. We should have run across the porch and down the dusty, narrow path lined with tall trees. Who cares if we ended up in the middle of nowhere. At least we would have been out of this house. Away from the sick fuck playing with our heads. Mentally torturing us. Warping our reality.

I take hold of Nina's bicep with tightening fingers. She glances up at me as I lean in and whisper in her ear.

"We need to go. Now. Something is beyond *off*. I can feel it."

Pulling back, Nina examines my face and eyes with her warring eyes. She weighs her desire to stay and help Jennifer versus abandoning her. The battle between head and heart. She wants to stay. It is written all over her face. To stand strong and fight to save the life crying from the other side of the door. Guilt will riddle her if she walks away and someone dies. Someone she could save.

But what if they are already dead?

Not once have I heard the screams, calls, or cries driving her to help. There is no way it's humanly possible she could hear a person scream for help while I do not. No human I have ever met has a pitch or tone or voice vibration only one other person hears. This whole situation has *bad news* written all over it.

She stares at the door a moment longer before facing me —undecided. She repeats this again and again before I squeeze my hand tighter and signal her to decide. I don't think we have much time left and she needs to choose. Glancing at the door one more time, her face bunches between her brows.

When she faces me again, the growls on the other side of the door get louder. Claws scratch the wooden floor nonstop. Any moment, they will tear through the thin timber.

"We need to go. *Now.*"

Nina nods and we run down the hall in the direction of the front door. We dart past the table and chairs in the dining room and hook a right toward the foyer. I grab the door handle and twist the knob, but it doesn't budge. *Fuck!* After a few forceful yanks, the door jerks open and the tree-lined pathway comes into view.

Thank god!

We walk out the door, onto the wooden-planked porch and down the steps toward the path. As soon as our feet hit the earth, both of us bend at the waist, slap our hands on our knees, and wheeze. Although five other people are stuck in that house, right now, I don't give a shit. Relieved doesn't even remotely begin to cover what I feel. Knowing I am no longer a prisoner in those walls… my freedom is a pair of wings soaring in the clouds.

My eyes pop open as I catch my breath and stand tall. Straighter than I have in the last twenty-four hours. When I glance over at Nina, I see so much fear carved in the lines of her face. Her eyes prickle with unshed tears. I put a reassuring hand on her arm and trace up and down her bicep over and over.

"It's okay. We're out. Everything will be fine now."

Her worried eyes invade my vision as she shakes her head more and more vigorously. I try to calm her. Soothe her. Tell her that everything will be okay and that we should probably start looking for help.

Her mouth opens and shuts. No words come out. Trying to encourage, I coax her to speak up. She tries again—her lips part as her mouth longs to vocalize, but nothing comes out. She does this three more times before finally I hear her voice.

"Not outside," she pants.

Her words are low. Barely a whisper. But I hear them. Loud and clear. And confusion infiltrates me. For a moment, I wonder if I misheard her. We are outside. So why would she say that? We stepped out on to the porch. I remember my feet hitting the dirt trail. The smell of moss and pine and earth. Cool, damp air coating my skin and refreshing my lungs.

We have to be outside.

We have to be.

Taking a step back, I give my periphery more girth. I

take in more than Nina's tear-stained face. And I see it now. I see what she sees.

Absent are the tall, richly-scented trees. Vanished is the dirt-coated pathway which trailed between them. The unlit porch leading up to the house—gone. The chirping cicadas and hooting owls nowhere to be found. Every last atom and molecule of the outside world—gone.

Only one thing stands in front of me.

Now, all I see is a door.

The door we ran from.

The door which lured Nina back in with the screams of an unknown woman. An unknown woman whose cries I cannot hear. An unknown woman who may or may not actually be on the other side. A door separating us from the sounds of snarls and growls and claws and teeth.

And possibly our demise.

Before I realize what is happening, I hear the deadbolt on the door click. The growls grow louder. A hollowness erupts in my belly. I scream, *"Run!"*

Everything moves in slow motion. We both run toward the dining room as the door at the end of the hall opens. The hinges creak in protest. Two large, black dogs exit. Their feet scramble against the grain as they attempt to gain traction and speed our way.

The bedroom door at the front of the hall is open and I run inside as quickly as possible. When I turn to see if Nina made it in before I slam the door shut, anguish takes hold of me.

Because what is happening in front of me can never be unseen. The very definition of how nightmares form and root deep in your psyche. A sight which will haunt me for the rest of my life.

In the middle of the hallway, the two dogs hold their ground. Each weighing more than a two-hundred-pound man, easily. Teeth bared and piercing Nina's flesh. Clamped on to her ankles as they drag her to the room at the end. Blood spurts from her Achilles and leaves a thick, red trail on the wood as they haul away her body. Her eyes plead for help as I reluctantly close the door.

As I abandon her.

In an attempt to save myself.

CHAPTER FOURTEEN

BELINDA

As soon as the door clicks shut, the screams and wails of pure terror surround me. My pulse whooshes deafeningly in my ears. My breath expands and contracts in hyperactive bursts. Sobs rattle every bone in my body. A never-ending stream of tears paints my cheeks. At any moment, I might detonate. Internally combust from fear of what lies on the other side of the door.

Nina's piercing howls penetrate every molecule in the air and crawl into my bloodstream. I shiver as her hands slap the floor and her nails dig into the wood. Scraping and clawing as she begs for her life. A dog growls a split-second before Nina yelps in pain. The blood-curdling combination echoes down the hallway, slithers under the door, and bleeds in my ears. Her shrill gurgle as she bawls my name —calls for my help—causes a new wave of tears.

But I stand locked in place. My feet refuse to move an inch.

No matter how much I will my legs to take a step forward and open the door, I don't. No matter how much I tell myself to help the woman on the other side of the door,

I don't. My heart tells me to open the door and help her while my brain rejects the notion.

Bam! Bam! Bam!

Fists and nails claw the outside of the door. Before I comprehend what just happened, a long, drawn out squeal slides down the door. I picture Nina reaching for the door-knob, but not having the wherewithal to grab hold. Seconds later, a blood-curdling scream stabs my ears and I slap my hands over them and press down.

Right now, Nina is inches away. The two of us separated by an inch-and-a-half piece of painted wood. She paws at the door as I simply stand here with hands pressed to my ears and hum to mask the pain of listening to her die.

Snarls rip louder as the two canines battle over their prize. Gnashing their teeth in a show of dominance. Nina's yelps soften as exhaustion takes over her body. As two vicious beasts have a pissing contest. Her body shadows the light under the door and I cry harder.

Then I see the unthinkable.

Two fingers. Between the floor and base of the door. Bright red and saturated with fresh blood. As the tips of her fingers squirm beneath the door, a floodgate of emotions ruptures inside me. Fear. Terror. Pain. Sadness. Loss. Worry. More for the woman who pleas for her life. Yet, also for myself as I desperately wish to save her, but am terrified of losing my own life in the process.

If only I could see through the door.

If only I knew what happened out there. Where the masochistic beasts stood.

Then I might consider opening the door. If I could safely help her, I would yank her in and slam the door shut.

But only if I stood a chance.

Squatting down, I grab the tips of her fingers. Wanting her to know I'm still here. Wanting her to know how sorry I am this is happening to her. How sorry I am for not waiting a second longer. For not waiting until she made it into the room. And how sorry I am for not having the courage to open the door and pull her inside with me.

That I'm sorry I didn't listen to her when she suggested I run for help.

Why didn't I listen to her?

If I would have run the first time we got the door open, we might both be safe right now. She might not be trapped in the hallway, struggling to survive. I might not be in this room as she begs for her life. I am a goddamn coward for closing the door early. Now, I listen to Nina take her final breaths.

I caress her fingers under the door as best I can. Blood coats my fingers where they touch hers. Guilt washes over me as a new wave of tears spills down my cheeks with abandon.

I lay on the floor and scoot closer to the door, my cheek pressed to the cold, dingy floor. As I stare at the small gap beneath the door, our eyes meet and I read the fear on her face. Her eyes blink rapidly as her lips twitch and chin wobbles. She gasps for breath just before she closes her eyes and a tear rolls over the bridge of her nose.

"I'm so sorry," I whisper. My words slip under the door.

When my apology grazes her ears, a torrent of sobs wracks her body.

We lay still—eyes connected—as sobs and silent wishes are exchanged between us.

A moment of clarity strikes when I no longer hear the dogs. No longer see their shadows. A new wave of hope floods me as I scramble upright.

"Hang on, I'm coming, Nina."

Hand on the knob, I start to twist and prepare myself to reach out and drag her in quickly. When the door latch clicks, Nina screams hysterically. "Don't open the door!" I freeze and wonder why she stopped me.

What is out there? Is she saving me? It should be the other way around.

"No, Nina. I need to pull you in while I can," I explain.

Her breathing shallows as she whimpers. "You can't save me. If they don't finish me off, I'll bleed out. And it won't take long. Either way, there's nothing you can do."

I want to call her a liar. Prove her wrong. Tell her if I pull her in, maybe I can stop the bleeding. How there is potential to save her life. But my mouth remains glued shut as I'm rendered mute.

I swallow the lump in my throat and plead with her again. But with each crack in my voice, I sound less and less convincing. "Shouldn't I at least try?"

Tears fall like fat raindrops from my chin. How do I give up? How do I leave her out there to die? Alone. I just can't. Not like this.

I grab the doorknob again and twist. When it reaches as far right as it'll go, I slowly open the door. At a measured pace, my eyes dart in every direction. A creak startles me as the hinges rub. The gap widens and an inch of the hall comes into view.

Nina lies at my feet—clothes tattered and blood-stained —with visible puncture wounds on her limbs and torso. My stomach drops. My lungs burn as I forget how to breathe. And the chambers of my heart work overtime as I admonish myself for not waiting a moment longer.

Selfish, selfish, selfish.

As I open the door another inch, her eyes widen and dart to mine instantaneously. She doesn't blink. Doesn't say a word. Just trembles. Shakes her head so quickly and subtly. Then, she screams. "Close the door! And don't come out. It's not safe."

I ignore her and open the door wider, ready to reach out and grab her. As soon as I extend my hand, a throaty growl rips through the air. A signal of ownership.

Deep guttural snarls reverberate on my left—the only part of the hall not visible until the door is ajar. Two massive, beast-sized dogs stand guard. Hackles raised. Teeth bared. Saliva drips like a leaky faucet from their mouths. Charged and ready to pounce. To take what rightfully belongs to them.

I slowly lower my hand and reach for Nina's arm. The closer I get, the more vicious and louder they become. If it's possible to grab her hand or arm, all I have to do is yank her in and close the door. Swiftly.

Slipping my hand around hers, I wobble in place as giddiness consumes me. *I will save her.* She is in my grasp. I have her. Everything will be okay. This will work.

My eyes shift away from the dog and I stare directly at Nina. Silently, I try to reassure her everything will be okay. And for a split-second, we share solace. A small moment of comfort.

But the solace and comfort fades as quickly as a camera flash.

As I tug her tired, battered body into the room, movement in my periphery catches my attention. Everything happens too fast for my brain to react.

A dog bolts to her other side, clamps down on her ankle and crushes her Achilles. The other dog lunges for her thigh, sinks its teeth into the muscle and thrashes. Blood spurts from her flesh and sprays the hall.

I tug her arm and try to break her free, but their grip strengthens. Both thrash vigorously as they tear at her flesh, slowly shredding her limb.

I can't watch this. Nina and I lock eyes, I apologize for everything I haven't done to save her. For everything I can no longer do. She gives me a slight nod and releases my hand, allowing the mammoth-sized beasts to rip her apart by the limbs.

I drop my hold on Nina. "Sorry," I whisper, then slam the door shut. I lean against the door and slide down until my ass hits the floor. Screams float in the air as Nina's body is torn apart. The tear of flesh. The rip of sinew. Bones crunching. Blood pools beneath the door. Her screams steadily fade as her mind can no longer bear the pain.

When the gruesome sounds subside and the hall falls silent, I cry harder. I cry for the woman I wasn't able to save. I scream at the sick fuck who does this to people and believes it is acceptable. And then I go silent, curious as to what will happen next.

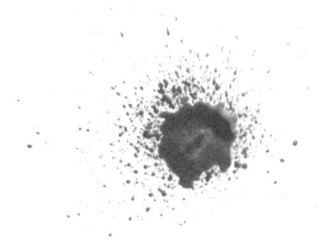

CAPTOR

God, that was fucking amazing.

I have never seen such magnificence. Such obedience. Such loyalty. My bitches will be eating like queens tonight. After all these years, after all the people I have laid out before them, they are subservient beyond measure.

Devoted to me.

Their master.

My love for them beyond measure.

Watching them tear her flesh. That first initial gush of my favorite hot, scarlet liquid. The fluidity. The rush as it spills and pools on the floor. A high that magnifies the ache between my thighs. Watching the spurts and sputters and oozing never gets old. Never grows familiar. The euphoria is different—new—every time it enters my bloodstream. Each hit more addictive than the previous. More delicious.

I slide my hand down my chest and slip my fingers between my legs—dire need to satiate the growing hunger inside me. The intensifying hunger at watching each of them die at my hand. *God!* My body is a lit electrical grid. A hum buzzes from the top of my crown, down my spine, across my chest and inundating my arms until it lands in my fingertips. It slithers down my torso and vibrates between my hips before dipping low in my legs and spreading through my feet to my toes. A shiver rolls throughout my body and I welcome the heady feeling.

The ache to witness my bitches tear someone limb from limb again is powerful. Potent. Has me eager to see the hunger in their eyes when I deliver the signal only their sensitive ears hear. The signal which tells them to dismember. But I also have the ability to instantly stop them with a different tone. To make them patiently wait on the sidelines and potentially lure out the abandoner who left Nina in the hall to die. The fear etched on Belinda's face when it dawns on her my bitches were just out of sight and obeying my command to stand down is priceless. And the dread widening her eyes when I command them to attack once more and finish the job is unparalleled.

I need the fear permanently carved on her face. To memorize it.

I want to jam-pack the last moments of her frivolous and meaningless existence with torture and pain and suffering.

And she needs to connect the dots and know her fate is sealed and will be delivered soon.

But the only way to do this is to show her. Show her and watch as realization dawns. The exact moment when she registers she has mere minutes left. Watch as the panic takes center stage and consumes every ounce of her flesh.

The more fear, the better.

I want to see it. Smell it. Hear it. Taste it. And later... *feel* it.

Absorbing how her senses perceived the fear in my own way.

Showtime, baby.

I sit in my chair and wiggle to adjust myself. To help ease the pent-up energy pooling between my thighs. Leaning forward, I rest my fingers atop the button on the microphone in front of me. Inhaling deeply, I mentally prepare for one of my favorite parts. The end.

I press the button and a loud crackle vibrates from the speakers—in this room as well as every other room in the house—as I blow on the mic's metal mesh. My exhalation into the mic rumbles throughout the house.

"Hey there, Belinda," I coo.

On the monitor, she tenses as her eyes dart left to right and left again. She scoots across the floor until she backs herself into the closest corner, then draws her legs to her chest and hugs them with shaky arms. She pants and rocks back and forth. Her mood shift has the corners of my lips curving up wickedly.

Now let's see how much fun I can have before I need my final dose.

"Glad you didn't step into the hall to save Nina from my bitches. Would have created a whole new set of problems for you. But we no longer need to worry about such things.

No, what you need to consider is how you are *it*. *The lone wolf*."

I pause. Give her a minute to register what I said. Wait for the reaction to pop on her face when recognition hits. The exact second when she realizes she is the only person left in the house. And how the house is no longer playing tricks on her. No longer messing with her head or making her see falsehoods.

Five breaths later and it smacks her in the face like a cast-iron skillet. Starting a mental domino effect. Once one falls, they all fall. In perfect harmony.

She gasps and tucks her head between her chest and knees. Her rocking shifts. Becomes more erratic and frenzied.

"That's right. You're it. You're the only one left. Everyone else—Skip, Billie, Kristen, Jennifer, Kelly, and Nina—is dead. And not too long from now, you will sit side by side with them. But before that happens, I have a present for you. A reward, if you will. Congratulations, you made it to the end. To be honest, I wasn't sure you would make it to the end."

I pause and let my confession sink in.

"When I watched you struggle over the decision to leave or not, with the front door wide open, I had no clue what choice you'd make. I hoped and prayed for you to stay. And my prayers were answered. So interesting to watch you wrestle between wanting to do the right thing and stay with Nina—to save someone who was already dead, by the way—or to walk out that door and run for the hills. I'll clue you in on something. If you would have walked out the door right then, you would have been free."

Belinda stops rocking and lifts her head at this. Eyes wide. Tears staining her cheeks.

"You could have run through the trees and come face to face with the street or one of the nearby neighbors. But savior complex won. I hoped and wished for this inevitable result, and it worked. You see, when I did my homework on you, I learned how easily you help strangers. Learned about your selflessness. Which is a worthy character trait. But is your pitfall. Your undoing. Because now… time is all you have left. Not much, in case you wondered. As you listen to the second hand tick on, I will give you your reward. Shall we call it a trip down memory lane?"

Wiggling the computer mouse, the arrow skirts across the screen and hovers a moment before I click. A television in the room Belinda sits in comes to life. The screen a bright blue until the feed starts.

"I've compiled a nice movie for you to watch. A memento, of sorts, for me, but a bit of insight for you. Just know, your fate is set in stone. But everyone's fate looks different."

She starts to rock in the corner again—her head shaking back and forth, hair flinging side to side. Even if she doesn't look up and watch the sweet compilation I created, she will *hear* it. Each and every act. She won't be able to tune it out or shut it off. I have control of the television—the display, the sound, the power. Nothing she does will stop it once I press start.

Clicking on the screen, I adjust the television volume.

Crank it loud and turn on the surround sound. I retrieve the current video file and add Nina's clip to the end. With a few tweaks, it is ready for takeoff. But before I press play, something catches my eye on the right screen.

In the live video feed, I hear mumbling. Belinda's body still works the same fevered rock—toes push off the floor, body rocks back, momentum dies down, weight shifts forward, toes push her back once more to continue the cycle. I turn up the volume on the live feed, trying to decipher the jumbled nonsense streaming from her lips.

"I'm going to get out of here. I'm going to make it. I'm going to survive this. I want to live."

I can't see her face or expression, but I hear the words clear as day with the volume turned up. She chants the same four lines repeatedly. As if saying them again and again will render them true.

Sorry, sweetheart. No one leaves alive.

No one.

I grant her a moment to sit there and reassure herself. Allow her to believe, even for the smallest blip of time, she has the ability to be saved. To be rescued. But I have other ideas. Plans assembled long before I brought any of them here.

I always have a plan. Always.

And if something goes astray, I have backup measures. Every single possibility carefully plotted before any of them arrive. This house—only I know the true appearance. This house—which has changed appearance several times— even if someone did escape, no one would find it as described. None of my victims would guess the outward appearance based on the interior.

Then again, who would dare return here. No one.

If someone did escape, why would they come back? The memories would be enough to mentally torture someone for the rest of their life. The screams and bloodshed, the isolation and captivity. If someone escaped and returned, they would *never* leave again. Of that, I would be one hundred percent certain.

One other factor comes into play... no one knows who I am.

Sure, they all sat down in a kumbaya circle and talked about the last things they remembered before waking up here, but none of them ever saw *me*. It was me who surveilled them for long periods of time. But I wasn't the one who rendered them unconscious. And I wasn't the one who dragged their body into a vehicle. My body didn't sit behind the steering wheel and drive them to this place. Someone else carried their bodies inside. For me. To do as I please.

Those men... a few trusted individuals I paid handsomely in ways that satisfied their needs. As well as my own. Not everyone requires monetary payment. Some are satisfied with simply watching what I do. Others have physical satisfaction requirements. None of them, however, want money. In a way, they are my sick and twisted henchmen. Willing to do anything I ask of them, as long as I give them what they desire in return. We have shared a beautiful relationship for several years.

My eyes flick back to the screen, to the brunette who

believes she will make it out of this house alive, and I have to rein in my excitement. Have to tamper down how badly I want to end her life right now. I take a deep breath and remind myself all good things come to those who wait.

I click play and the blue screen on the television switches to the initial image of the video. Adrenaline shoots through my bloodstream like an electrical current. Not only will she have the pleasure of witnessing what happened to the others, but I also get a replay.

Which lights my skin on fire.

The first segment pops up on the screen—Skip and Billie in the second bedroom. Kisses exchanged while hands grope like teenagers. Skip was a sex fiend who believed he was the greatest gift to womankind. Billie was a frail little girl who wanted love however she could get it, in any capacity. They were the perfect match. A match I took my time mastering.

Belinda presses her head to her knees as Billie and Skip orgasm on screen. She shoves her fingers in her ears and hums to ignore the sound. But I know she hears it. The volume is cranked up. Anyone within five hundred feet would hear it clear as day.

Their moans die down and all you hear is their heavy breaths. Then it happens. The moment when Skip felt the effects of what I laced the condom with. Belinda's head shoots up. Her interest piqued as she hears Skip and Billie talk. Billie asking Skip if he is okay. Skip shrugging her off while he silently freaks out.

The rest of his demise happens so quickly.

Belinda watches as Skip's body slowly goes into paralysis and collapses over Billie. His limbs don't move. His body weight crushes her. She watches as Billie struggles to get out from underneath him. As she, too, crawls into a corner and rocks in fear. As she hears Skip's body gasp its last opportunity for breath.

Now she's paying attention.

Belinda rises from the floor and moves to the bed, garnering herself a better view of the television. The look in her eyes startles me. She seems more intrigued—enticed—than I originally anticipated. Perhaps she has a dark side I had not uncovered. A deep need to watch others suffer and perish.

Color me fascinated.

The video continues to play. Billie dresses herself, ready to escape the room, as if Skip dying was no big deal. When Billie walks into the hall, I study Belinda closely. Ready to scrutinize her reactions and body language as she witnesses the next fatality.

She stares at the screen. Eyes glued to Billie as she runs along the endless hallway. I count down the seconds, waiting and watching Belinda as I know what happens in… five, four, three, two, one.

Belinda's head jerks back, but her body stays put. No fear. No disgust. No anxiety. No tears.

Completely emotionless.

Hmmm. "What do we have here?" Maybe Belinda is more like me than she is willing to admit. Maybe death and dismay are as fascinating and thrilling to her as they are to me. All I want is to see her every reaction now. Maybe she is worthy of staying.

The video drones on and images of Kristen and Jennifer in the kitchen pop up. Kristen is working on more food while Jennifer cuts the peanut butter and jelly sandwich. Belinda leans in closer and tilts her head to the side as she gazes at them while they chitchat in the kitchen.

My eyes fixate on Belinda again while I wait to see how she reacts to Kristen versus the toaster oven.

Kristen grabs the plug and her body starts to shake and stiffen at the same time. As thrilled as I am to watch the replay, I can't help but watch as Belinda seems enthralled by the whole scenario. Completely transfixed and, seemingly, wanting more.

As the light vanishes from Kristen's eyes, Belinda rises from the bed and steps closer to the screen. Mesmerized.

I'm in awe.

The screen flickers to Jennifer in the living room, crying until she feels a pang in her gut. Belinda takes another step closer to the television, arms crossed over her chest as she leans in. Eyes vacant as she watches Jennifer make her way to the bathroom.

Another step closer.

Jennifer's nose bleeding heavily before she clutches her stomach. Moments later, getting herself onto the toilet. Her body revolting from both ends. Belinda ogles with pure fascination as Jennifer shakes and convulses. Her gaze doesn't falter as Jennifer collapses on the floor in her own vomit, foam erupting from her mouth and excrement from the other end. Jennifer's eyes roll back and she thrashes violently. Belinda steps closer, but distance remains between her and the screen.

And then it ends and Belinda's shoulders relax slightly.

Is she relieved?

The next image on the screen includes her. I'm quite anxious for her reaction. Belinda cocks her head to the side in interest. Kelly wakes up and looks around the room before heading for the door. Kelly slaps a hand over her stomach when she smells food cooking.

Belinda steps closer again and follows Kelly as she creeps toward the bedroom exit and steps out of the room. She makes her way to the empty kitchen and spots the vat of bubbling food. After Kelly takes a few steps, the kitchen morphs and becomes desolate.

Another step closer.

Kelly wanders through the newest version of the house and tries to find anyone else. She walks with a single candle, and an air of concern etched in her expression. When Kelly steps back into the room where she, Belinda, and Nina were sleeping and finds it empty, Belinda's eyes bulge.

Fascinating.

Kelly looks around the room and notices the only items left in the room are my most prized possessions. As soon as Belinda notices this, her eyes shoot up to them on the wall. For a moment, her eyes dance back and forth between the screen and the shelves.

Right foot forward.

Kelly squats down to pick up the note I left, opening the envelope and reading it. I zoom in on the note and give Belinda an opportunity to see it.

Belinda stares on as Kelly has surmised her own fate

and tries to run. But when she does, there is only one option left. Kelly goes through that fateful door. Belinda appears entranced as Kelly is taken captive. Transfixed as Kelly sees the pile of bodies in the room she cannot escape. Drawn closer as she sees me—completely disguised in black—step forward and cut off Kelly's pleas as she barters for her life. Glued to the screen when I begin the process of vanquishing my prey.

Never once does her face slip, falter or shy away. She wants to see it all. Wants to watch how I take their lives.

And then the screen flickers to the next image.

Her and Nina.

The two of them by the front door, neither leaving.

It is now when she hangs her head a moment before watching the two of them. Every fleeting second from the moment they stuck together to the moment when Nina took her last breath.

She doesn't get closer to the screen. Doesn't utter a word. Doesn't show any emotion. Simply remains stoic.

When the video stream ends, I click the television off and observe Belinda a moment. She stands there, unmoving and lifeless. Expression blank. She may have been captivated, but she is definitely not like me. I now know this to be certain. If she were like me, her face would have lit up like a meteor shower when it ended. Her body would jolt to life with the desire and hunger for more. Her mouth would open and ask to see it again and again.

But she did none of these things.

Which means her fate is most definitely sealed.

CHAPTER FIFTEEN

BELINDA

FROZEN IN PLACE, I cannot believe what I just watched. Cannot believe all of that actually happened. I mean, I know Nina died exactly how I saw it… again, but it cannot *all* be real.

Can it?

After all, whoever brought us here has been screwing with our heads the entire time. What if this video is doctored? What if it is another attempt at messing with me? Nina died less than an hour ago, but that doesn't mean what happened to the others on the video was real.

Or does it?

Right now, nothing is certain. Everything is so distorted; I don't know left from right. Up from down. Back from front. This whole place is one crazy house of mirrors. One illusion after another. Rooms altering appearances in the blink of an eye. Furniture in place one second and gone the next. The house rundown then pristine then crumbling to pieces.

What is real anymore?

Not sure I am a good judge of reality anymore. Feels like

one crazy, long nightmare. Maybe I will wake up any second and life will be normal. I'll be wrapped in my comforter, drenched in sweat but relieved to learn this was all one freakishly weird dream.

I close my eyes, squeeze them tightly, and block out any light in the room. Taking a few deep breaths, I tell myself this is just a dream. That it cannot possibly be real. After chanting the mantra in my head again and again, I open my eyes and pray what I see is my own bedroom. Pray this is a bad dream brought on by watching too many horror movies.

But I am sorely disappointed.

When I open my eyes, I am still in this godforsaken place. With some twisted son of a bitch who gets his or her jollies from killing people. Someone who probably fantasizes about death. Maybe even masturbates to the idea.

Sick fuck!

Well, I refuse to play the victim. Refuse to *become* the victim.

I will get out of here. One way or another.

I recall the first time we all gathered in the living room and tried to figure out a way to leave this place. How we all went to different rooms and tried to open doors and windows. Tried to break them. At that point, nothing worked.

When it was only me and Nina, we got the door open. Things had changed. This place had changed.

So, maybe I should try again.

I study the wall opposite the bedroom door. The wall with two small windows shrouded in curtains. Since the last house shift, maybe the windows changed. Like the front door, maybe they have vulnerabilities.

I walk over to the closest window and draw back the shabby curtain. The window coated with grime and no longer transparent. But transparency doesn't matter. What matters is if the window will open. Or if the glass will break.

I unlatch the window lock, drop my hand to the base of the frame, and take a deep breath. *Please, please, please let this work. Let this window open.*

One more deep breath and I push up on the exhale. Relief and excitement flood my veins as the window slides up. Slowly, the window opens fully. Internally, I scream with joy.

I'm getting out of here.

But then I focus on what is in front of me. The second I comprehend it all, my stomach lurches.

No!

In front of me, just past the window's mesh screen, is a set of iron bars. I pop the screen out and wrap my hands around the cold, damp metal and shake with every ounce of power I possess.

They don't budge.

Running my hands along the bars, I feel for a latch or lock. Something to unhook and push the bars open. But I come up short. In fact, the bars seem welded together at the seams. No cracks. No breaks. Nothing usable to rip the barrier away. At least not on this window.

Hurriedly, I switch to the other window and follow the same process. And once again, another set of bars barricade me in. With no imperfections in the metal. But I won't let this deter me. There are several windows in this house, plus the front door. If I have to, I will try each and every one of them. I refuse to give up. Refuse. I won't let this lunatic control me.

I will get out of here.

And I will go home.

I run out of the bedroom and head for the room down the hall. I go through the same process with both windows in this room and end up with the same result. But it's okay. There are still more windows.

Never give up.

Never cave.

Right?

Room by room, I check each window. At this point, I'm practically ripping the curtains from each window. Can't be many windows left in the house, but I refuse to believe none will let me escape. I have to believe I am not meant to die in this house of mind games. Have to believe I will get out. That I am destined to live a long and happy life. And I will eventually forget this happened.

I have to.

When I get to the last window, I draw back the curtains and stare a moment before closing my eyes.

This is it. This is the one. You will get through this window and out of this place. You will get saved. You will be safe.

I open my eyes and suck in a breath. My fingers skim to the window locks and pop them open. My hands glide down the glass and grip the ledge of the metal base.

This is it.

The moment of truth.

I push up on the window and audibly exhale when the cool night air paints my skin. I pop out the window screen and freeze before reaching out to the ominous iron bars.

Please, God. Let this be it. Let this be the one. The one which grants me my freedom. I will do anything you ask. Please, please, please! I beg of you.

I extend my hands and my fingertips connect with the cold, solid barrier. I grip the iron until my knuckles whiten, take a deep breath, and send a silent prayer to whoever listens. *Please, let this work.* I thrust my weight forward and back a few times, but drop my head when the bars don't budge.

It's okay. Maybe there is a crack or a break. Something to work with.

I trace my hands up and down each bar. Skim my fingers along the top and bottom. Nothing. They are absolutely, positively stuck in place.

A tear slips from my eye as I choke back the emotion lodged in my throat. Any second, the floodgates will rip wide open. I let go of the bars and lay my hands on the windowsill. I can't take this anymore. The games. The torture. The playful hell this person has put me, and six others, through.

And then a bomb detonates inside me. Slowly spreading from head to toe. Cell by cell, I ignite into a raging inferno. Fury and hatred consume every thought I possess. I'm done. Over this asshole. This piece of shit who decided to take my life and throw it in the trash. As if I don't matter.

As if I have no say, no voice. As if they get to decide. As if they make the rules.

As if they are God.

Well, I say… "Fuck you."

The words fall easily from my lips. The menace laced in those two words—those seven letters—states exactly how I feel. Royally pissed off.

I lower my head an inch so my face is center with the window and take a moment. The breeze brushes against my skin and invigorates me. Gives me courage. Someone, somewhere, will hear me. I have to believe it.

I inhale and exhale deeply a few times and brace for what I'm about to do.

Drawing in one last breath, I close my eyes and hope someone hears me. On the exhale, I scream at the top of my lungs. Belting out to the world beyond this place. Not caring who hears it as long as it's someone outside this hellhole.

I scream for help. Repeat the word as loudly as possible and as often as possible.

The release is intense and heady and exhilarating. I cry out into the night like a banshee over and over.

Then, a loud bang detonates farther inside the house. Then another. And another. Like an oversized domino effect.

Bam! Bam! Bam!

And then it hits me. I belt out louder cries for help. As loud and lengthy as my lungs and larynx will allow. I scream as if my life depends on it. As if I will die any minute if someone doesn't hear my cries and rescue me.

And just as I am about to belt out another scream, the window in front of me slams shut. The locks bolt into place. Every ounce of light vanishes.

Officially in the darkest of darks.

Unable to see my own hand in front of my face. The anger and the rage flowing freely a moment ago is gone. Nowhere to be found.

Now? Now, terror takes hold.

I step forward as my hands blindly move side to side in front of me, trying to locate a wall or piece of furniture. Seven steps later, I land on a wall and skim the surface until I reach a corner. It is here where I find refuge. It is here where I twist so my back is to the corner. I slide down the wall until my butt hits the floor. This is where I will be safest because no one can sneak up behind me. And this is where I will sit and wait for someone to come rescue me.

Please let someone have heard my screams. God, Buddha, Allah, Ganesha, Zeus—all the deities of the universe. Please give me a sign. Let me know someone heard me. That someone will help me. That I will get to leave this hellhole. This prison. Please, please, please!

I sit in absolute silence. The only sound comes from my heavy breaths and raging pulse beneath my ear. Seconds become minutes. Minutes turn into hours. And I have no idea how much time has passed, but it feels as if I have sat in this corner for years. Feels as if I am deteriorating, molecule by molecule—crumbling to ash with each tick of the second hand.

A loud bang ripples through the air. A detonation which

has me scooting back into the corner farther. Has me scared to know the source of said booming.

When it goes quiet for a few minutes, I crawl forward a foot or two in the hopes of glimpsing the source.

I squint into the darkness when something catches my eye.

But then I freeze, unsure what to do. I contemplate inching closer to see what shines brightly nearby, but don't. Fear roots me in place. My lungs burn, and I remind myself to breathe. My pulse skyrockets as adrenaline shoots through my veins.

Somehow, I garner the strength to stand. Inch by inch, I walk with purpose. Toward the object of my desire. I don't look away. If I do, it might disappear. My feet are boulders as I trudge across the room. Halfway there and it feels as if I have walked miles.

Without warning, bright lights illuminate the room. I squint, but keep my eyes open slightly. Fearful what I see will vanish. I step closer. Needing to see if this is real. Feet away, causing a rainstorm of tears to stream down my face.

Thank you, God.

I blink back the tears as I stand and stare at my way out. As I stare out the open front door. And my way home.

CHAPTER SIXTEEN

BELINDA

Is this real? Am I actually going to get out of here?

The door is ajar. Maybe twenty or thirty feet away from me. The trees lining the dusty path outside call out to me. Beckon me to bolt out the door and escape into the night.

So why haven't I moved yet? Why are my feet rooted in place? Why am I not sprinting to my freedom?

One simple word... *Fear.*

Fear this is a trap. Fear if I step another foot forward, something will jump out to get me. Fear if I walk through the door, I will be lost in the middle of nowhere and no one will ever find me. Fear I will not survive.

After everything that has happened, this seems way too easy.

Why now? Why would whoever brought us here suddenly decide to let me go? After all the games and death, what has changed? Is it because I'm the last one standing? Because I won't back down? That I *want* to keep fighting for my life?

When I was forced to watch the sick-as-hell video recap of each person dying before me, most of them had something in common. All except me and Nina. Everyone had given up trying to escape. It looked as if they all accepted being stuck here. Accepted the free amenities. Didn't question why someone would bring us all here—to a house stockpiled with food—and tell us to treat our time as if it were a vacation retreat.

I don't get it. Don't understand why people would be so willing to set aside the fact we were—I still am—trapped inside a house against our will. Sure, the door hangs wide open right now. But why? After killing six of us, why would I be so lucky as to be allowed to leave? Wouldn't whoever brought us here fear I would go to the authorities or the media and tell them my story? Wouldn't they fear being caught?

I want to step forward. Want to run out the door. Past the cozy patio furniture. Sprint down the path, through the trees, and scream at the top of my lungs. Run to the closest person, latch on to them and tell them how grateful I am to see another person. Then, I want to dash toward freedom and forget every single minute of being in this place.

But fear has me suspended in time. Glued to the floor.

This may be my only chance at survival. I can't let it slip through my fingers. Can't let this opportunity be for nothing. I have to at least try, *don't I?*

As much as I fear it, I close my eyes and take a deep breath. I try to center myself. Center my thoughts and focus. *I can do this. I will get out of here. I will go home.*

I inhale again and open my eyes. Focus on my goal. My escape. My way home.

I can do this.

I will do this.

I will get out of here.

My resolve locked and loaded; I tell myself it is time. Time to run and not look back. Time to run through the door, across the porch deck, down the dusty path and beyond the line of trees. I will get through this and then I can breathe. Breathe like I never have before.

Deep breath in, deep breath out.

I launch for the door. As exhausted as I am, my stride is swift and absolute. Twenty more feet. I inhale deeply. Ten more feet. The air escapes my lungs. I run past the door frame.

Yes!

The porch outside fades. Morphs into something else entirely. A second later, I am running through the middle of the living room.

"Nooooo!"

I slow down, eventually coming to a full stop where the living room and dining room meet. The back of my eyes sting with unshed tears. A wad of cotton clogs my throat.

I was there. I was outside of the house. How? Why? *Why?!*

I can't take the torture anymore. The searing pain in my chest. I look to my left and see the front door is still exactly as it was before—wide open. Open to taunt and punish me. Torture me. Tell me *you aren't going anywhere*. The hurt is a hot branding iron to my heart. The fear comes at me from every direction. As much as I don't want to give up, I feel it may be better if I did.

But I refuse to go down without a fight.

You may want to play your vicious little mind games with me, but I will definitely make you work hard if your goal is to take my life. And when I can no longer hold the tension in my body, I let go.

I tip my head back, stare up at the ceiling, and scream at the top of my lungs.

My scream carries no words. Only the pure rage echoing in my soul. Anger. Fury. Hatred. Fear. I belt it all out, as loud as I can for as long as I can. And when my scream ceases, I drag in another lungful of air and repeat the process all over again.

If this person is going to rob me of my life, I may as well make it known to anyone within earshot I am here and I am about to die. Why make it all too easy for this asshole. Why not make him or her sweat a little. Make them worry and wonder if anyone else hears me howling. Especially after my wails out of the window not long ago.

When my scream dies down, I go to suck in another breath and ready myself to belt out my next caterwaul. But nothing happens. My breath doesn't come. My inhale feels robbed. Empty.

I stare down at my body and pat my chest as I try to draw more oxygen into my lungs. With each attempt to drag air in, it feels as if there is no air. As if the atmosphere has been depleted. As if I am suddenly in a sealed chamber and the air has been withheld.

I start to panic. My lungs burn the more deprived they become. Again, I try to inhale. My body remembers how, but just doesn't. I get nothing. If anything, it feels as if the air is being *sucked out* of my lungs.

I gasp. My lungs on fire. Eyes pinched shut. Legs giving out as I crumble to the floor.

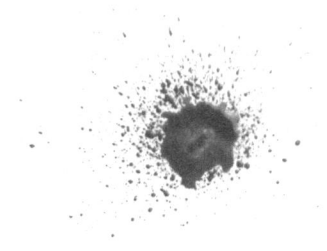

CAPTOR

She slows her stride as she reaches where the living and dining room meet. Confusion and frustration and sadness and anger register in the lines of her face. Have me leaning forward. But now that I'm closer, I read the actual hatred and undiluted rage in her eyes. Red with lividity.

That alone makes me squirm in my chair.

I love it when they fight. When they develop a false sense of hope. When they believe they have a fighting chance. But they have no chance. None whatsoever.

I decide.

I choose *who* comes here.

I choose *how* they come here.

I choose *when* they come here.

I choose *when* they die.

I choose *how* they die.

My choice.

Always.

Letting them believe they have a fighting chance… well, let's just say that is part of the dog and pony show. There is a reason I plan everything out. Why everything is exactly how it is. Why specific people are selected. I know exactly how they will behave and what they will inevitably do and how I will kill them. I study them for weeks. Sometimes months. Put them under a microscope and magnify every facet of their meaningless existence.

Easy as pie. *Which is a ridiculous saying because pie has never fucking been easy.* But I digress.

Suddenly, the speakers on my monitor squeal from her incessant screaming. She tips her head back and faces the ceiling while she heaves as much noise as possible. I reach over and press mute on the sound.

I'll give her a minute. Let her get her jollies while she screams for dear life. It doesn't matter, though. No one will hear her right now. The only scream anyone may have heard were those she belted out before I shut the windows. But I have checked the exterior cameras several times since and nothing flashes me warning signs.

Done with her first scream, she takes a moment and collects her breath. Then, I watch as she drags in another full breath and turns her head back toward the ceiling, screaming at the top of her lungs again.

Keep screaming, sweetheart. Not a soul will hear your cries.

I will allow her this one last cry of passion. But no more. After this, she won't utter a single, solitary sound. Matter of fact, she won't do much of *anything* after this. I will let her have this moment. Allow this catharsis. Maybe it will placate her. Make her feel as if she has the upper hand. Give her the impression someone will hear her and care enough to save her.

I will let her have this one last moment. Because that is exactly what this is. Her last moment. After this… she will belong to no one but me.

I reach over and pick up the last doll in the chair and hold it in my hands.

So precious. So beautiful. Such a glorious addition to my wall.

When this is all over, I will take my new, precious prizes and place them along the wall. They will sit in place, among the rest of my beauties, and keep me company and give me solace while I plan my next adventure.

I run my hand across the silky soft hair. My body trembles as I stroke the luxurious souvenir. I can't wait until they are all in their place and I can show them exactly how much I love them. How much I really wanted them in my world. How happy I am they will forever be a part of it.

Arousal stirs below my waist and I reach down and squeeze between my legs a little. I need to tame myself for now. Soon, it will be over. Soon, I will be able to relieve this lusty tension building and growing stronger since they all arrived. Soon, they will all sit on the shelf, eyes forward, and watch me as I ogle them. My hand squeezes harder at the thought.

I need this to happen sooner rather than later. Need my release. Need to be satiated.

As I focus back on the monitor, it appears as if Belinda's scream is coming to an end and she is prepping her lungs for another. Little does she know, that is not going to happen.

I wiggle the mouse so the arrow lands exactly where I want it. My finger hovers over the button, ready to click. Just as she is ready to suck in another deep breath, I press the mouse and activate the vacuum chamber function in the house. The vacuum which affects every room… except the one I currently sit in.

And it is exciting… this exact moment.

The grand finale.

Although I love watching each and every person trapped here die, the last person in each group is the pièce de résistance. The last one always heightens the thrill. Makes my heart pound a little bit harder than the rest. Causes my breath to hitch as they take their last. Drives the ache between my legs to a new plateau. A high like no other.

And right now, my body is soaring.

I lean forward and bite my lip as Belinda desperately tries to suck in air. Lines bunch her forehead. Eyes widen in pain—filled with questions no one can answer except me. Skin paling as her lungs search for a molecule of oxygen. But none will come. There will be no relief in sight. Soon, her pinked skin will ashen. And once she dies, it will transition to my favorite shade of blue.

I love that shade of blue more than anything.

Her hands fly to her throat. Her mouth stuck open in a frenzy as she keeps trying to draw in air. For a second, I think how fun it would be to give her air again. Just for a minute. To make her believe she passed a test. Let her believe she will survive. Let her believe she won't suffocate after all.

So, I do it. I shut off the vacuum mechanism and watch as excitement lights her eyes and her lungs drag in air. Deep gasps, one after another. Her relief is instantaneous.

But she doesn't realize I am toying with her. Doesn't know in another thirty seconds, I plan to suck the air from her lungs once more. Doesn't know I am giving her just a slight touch of hope. A glimmer. Letting her believe she will live. Before I yank it out from under her feet once more. And for the last time.

There will be no relief this go around.

Her breathing settles into a normal rhythm. Her skin returning to normal coloration. Relief written all over her face.

It is time.

And just as she appears as though she may belt out another cry for help, I hit the button for the last time. And just as quick, I show her she has absolutely no control over her own life anymore. I own her life. She belongs to me.

And that notion… it is *THE* most hedonistic feeling in the world.

To own someone.

To rule their life, their world.

To decide if and when and how their life will or will not continue.

To control every single aspect of their existence from a singular moment. Knowing that, if given the opportunity, they would bow down to you, or do absolutely anything, if it meant they would survive.

But survival is not why I bring them here.

I bring each and every one of my victims here to die.

I bring them here because they are flawed or ruined or harmful, to themselves or others.

I bring them here to eliminate them from the world. To take away any future chance of them passing on their traits or disease to someone else, whether or not intentionally.

They are the ones who deliver a burden to others. And burden comes in a variety of forms, but nevertheless it is still a feeling, an infliction, a physicality, a mental or emotional breakdown which will make the recipient wish they never had to deal with the other person. To worry about them. To think of them. To know they could be lingering at any given moment.

The manwhore who uses women like they have no other purpose other than pleasing him.

The desperate woman who will cling to any form of attention given to her, regardless of who it may hurt.

The frail and quiet woman who would rather be wrapped up in her work than explore the world.

The outgoing woman who lives and breathes and sleeps her job and never gets out into the thick of life to do anything else; never shares herself with anyone.

The smart-ass, lippy woman who believes she knows everything about everything and is convinced she is invincible to anything that comes at her.

The woman who wants to save everyone, who wants to be there for everyone—even when the attention is not wanted—and never considers sometimes it is *you* who needs saving.

And the woman who gives up her opportunity at freedom because guilt—in every situation in her life—weighs heavy on her shoulders for not doing more at all costs.

They may not all be indecent or horrible humans, but they bring down others in some way, shape, or form. Bring anguish into the heart or head or body of others. Make others concerned or worried or unhappy or angry. They are users and the used.

I peek up at the screen and take in Belinda. She is bent at the waist, knees slowly buckling. Body collapsing to the floor as her hands clutch her throat. Her face reddens once more and her eyes appear as if they want to burst from their sockets. A minute and a half has passed since I sucked the oxygen from the room. At most, she can only survive without it up to three minutes.

But I have a feeling she won't even make it to three.

I glance over at the second hand which ticks with a steady beat next to the computer. The rhythm soothes me like a metronome as I witness her work with every fiber, every molecule, every cell in her body to breathe the air no longer around her.

Two minutes and three seconds.

Her body plants face-first on the floor. Hands no longer clenching her neck. Body stiffening as the whites of her eyes turn red. The pressure in the room like gravity overload. Her body won't be able to handle much more.

Two minutes and thirteen seconds.

Her body goes rigid. Eyes wide open and unmoving. Mouth agape. Lips becoming purple along the plump, fleshy parts and edged with a thin blue. Skin losing its color and hinting at the pale color of organic cotton.

Two minutes and twenty-two seconds.

I will leave her there until a few seconds after the three-minute mark. Make sure there is not one ounce of survival left in her lungs or muscles. Make sure she wasn't able to hold a breath for any period of time in the beginning which I did not take note of.

Two minutes and forty-seven seconds.

Her face has sunken in. The suction of the vacuum draining every atom from her body. Her fleshy face now showing hints of a beautiful blue sky, a hint of clouds here and there.

Three minutes and seventeen seconds.

I deactivate the vacuum mechanism. With a few more mouse clicks, all of the windows and the front door open. The house floods with air from the outside world. Waiting another minute, I let the house fill with breathable air before I step out of the room.

And I am so ready to leave this room. Leave it and ogle over my final, precious plaything. Revel in the glorious rush which comes afterward. After they all die. My body aches with need and desire. Screams with excitement and victory. I don't think I will ever find something, anything, which eclipses this euphoria.

CHAPTER SEVENTEEN

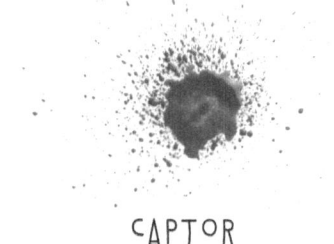

CAPTOR

I TWIST the doorknob and listen to the air crackle between the room and the hall as the airflow adjusts among the two spaces. I am eager to leave this room. Eager to see the last of seven laying on the floor. Eager to add a new set of dolls to the shelves on my walls.

Before exiting the room, I snag my cell phone and tablet —always ready in case a situation arises. I step into the hall and head to where Belinda's body lays peacefully on the floor. I round the corner and see her lying on the hardwood between the back of the couch and one of the dining chairs.

I approach with caution. Rolled on her side, she faces away from me. Until I see her face, I act as if anything is possible.

The wood creaks under me with each step I take—my pace leisure and measured. I step around the length of her body and walk along her front side, starting at her feet, and mentally prepare myself for every possible scenario. A few steps closer to her head and I am granted the gift of her pale blue cheeks and lips.

Heat blooms throughout my body. The finality of another group lights my insides like a nuclear bomb.

Unlocking my phone, I call the one person who matters most right now. My partner in crime. The one who gets his jollies as much as I do from these moments. "Hey," my breathy voice purrs. "It's done."

"All of them?" His voice is liquid sex in my ear.

"Every last one of them."

"I'll be there in a moment. Wait for me." His voice comes out raspy on the last three words.

The line goes dead as my phone drops the call. Been waiting this long already, what is another ten minutes. I stare at the female form in front of me and reach between my legs, my fingers pressing firmly against the ache.

The least I can do is drag the body back to be with the others.

Setting the tablet down and sliding the phone in my pocket, I fist Belinda's ankles and drag her body down the hall. She is a little heavier than the other women, but if I am able to drag a full-bellied man around, I can do the same with her.

As I haul her into the room, I hear the crunch of gravel in the back drive. Elation floods my veins as I jog out of the room and make my way to him. A door inside the kitchen— one kept hidden from all my special guests—opens and closes with barely a sound. I head toward it and halt when I step inside.

Ten feet away, I spot him. Dark hair, broad shoulders, lean, defined muscles, and a tall stature. He breathes desire and lust and carnality. I run to him and jump up, wrapping my legs around his waist and locking my arms securely behind his neck.

"Hey, babe. Happy to see me?" His question laced with sarcasm and loaded with cockiness.

I grind my hips on his. "You know I am."

His dark blue eyes turn molten and burn mine. "Are they all in there?"

I nod as my lips form the word *yes*, but not uttering a sound. One corner of his lips turns up, followed by the other, and slowly curves into the most delicious and sadistic smile. Over the years, I have grown to love him and his smile. He grabs my ass in both hands and walks.

"Hold on tight, babe."

He walks us out of the kitchen and I know exactly where we are headed. Down the hall, last door on the left. The room where they all lay spread across the floor. The room where we seal every mission with a final hurrah. The room where we absorb all the energy leaving their bodies and floating in the air.

He steps into the room and walks us over to the same space we celebrate each finality. The bed.

He throws me across the mattress and I squeal and giggle. He crawls onto the mattress—predator after prey—and stalks forward.

It has been far too long. And I need him to satiate the burn inside me. Need him to top off the energy transference and high I get every time I observe someone die at my hands.

He traces his hands up my legs and stops at my waistband, undoing the button and zipper. With a firm grip and a solid yank, my shorts and panties slide down my legs in a flash. He licks his way up my calf to my thigh until he reaches my apex. He lavishes me with his tongue and creates an electrical surge in my veins. On my skin.

I thrust toward his mouth, wanting more when he pulls away. He waggles his finger and clucks his tongue. "Be a good little girl and I'll reward you with more."

As he tugs his shirt over his head, my fingers drift south to the bundle of nerves between my thighs. *I need more.* He eyes my movement, groans, then bites his lower lip. Undressing with more enthusiasm, he yanks off his jeans and kicks them aside as his cock springs free.

I ogle every inch of his body and suck on my lower lip. He peeks over his shoulder at the seven people taken by my hands, then turns back to me. "Fuck, you turn me on. You, this…" He gestures behind him. "My dick is so fucking hard."

I trace my fingers up and down my slit and coat them with my arousal. Then, I reach up to wipe it on his cock. He hisses before lurching forward. Within seconds, his forearms cage me in and his hips rock forward, filling me with his thick cock.

This… right here, right now. This is an added bonus to the whole situation.

When I first started all of this, it was only me. I had to discover ways to lure people in. Learn how to drag them off and have my way with them. Sometimes it equaled sex. Sometimes not.

Which is how I found him. I needed another set of hands. Someone who would do some of the heavy lifting.

Someone who would help me pick more than small, frail women as my victims. Someone who would open up my world and make it much more alluring. Thrilling.

I observed him for more than a year. Studied his day-to-day living. Followed him to work and when he went out. Saw who he hung out with and what they did together. Majority of the time, he was a poster boy—always doing the right thing when everyone was nearby. But there was something about him. Something he didn't put out there for everyone to witness. Something only my eye would catch because it was familiar.

One night, after a few too many drinks at the bar, he walked to his car and stopped when he heard screams behind the building. He snuck around and caught some piece of shit raping a woman by the dumpster. Without a word, he grabbed the man's shirt, hauled him off of her, and beat the shit out of him until he was unrecognizable and no longer breathing.

The woman, higher than a kite, passed out and never saw his face.

Once he'd had a minute to process the whole situation, I paid close attention to his reaction. When a shit-eating grin lit up his face… I knew.

Stepping out of the shadows, I approached him and said I had an offer to make him. Was all downhill from there. Five years have passed since that night. Since he said yes to my proposal. Since he fucked me up against the dumpster to seal the deal. Since I branded my nails into his flesh until he bled. It was the most intoxicating moment in our history.

Now, with every victory we celebrate, we carry on the

ritual. We seal each group's death by fucking within feet of their bodies. By refueling this never-ending hunger in our blood. By satiating our need and ache and desire. The need to kill. The ache which slowly fills us as each perishes. The desire which courses through our bodies as each body hits the floor.

A yearning between us only we understand. A biological urge only we satiate for each other. A drive which will never stop or reach capacity.

He rocks back and slams forward, his weight forcing his thick cock to collide with my cervix. "Harder," I bite out. The word a growl in the back of my throat.

His hips piston faster as he adds more weight to the motion. *Fucking glorious.* I clamp down on his shoulders, curl my knuckles, and get ready to puncture his flesh and mark him as mine again.

He kisses along my jaw until he reaches my ear. "Do it, babe. Make me yours," he begs.

Not as if he would ever belong to anyone else; and vice versa.

I sink my nails into his flesh—nails I keep long and manicured and pointy like talons. He hisses between his teeth and bites the tender flesh where my neck meets my shoulder. With slow precision, I drag my nails down the length of his torso with firm and steady pressure the entire way. When I reach his ass, I retract and bring my nails to the upper midline of his back, on either side of his spine, and repeat the same action.

"Fuck, yes!" he growls.

He pumps inside me harder and faster. The bed slams

against the wall over and over. Clapping to the rhythm of our fucking. My body incinerates with each thrust. He throws my ankles over his shoulders and jackhammers in and out of me. I trail my hands down his back and paint my fingers in his hot blood. Coated, I bring them to my lips and smear the red-hot heat over my lips. As he watches this, his cock flinches and further hardens inside me. In the blink, he fucks me with abandon.

"Jesus fuck, I fucking love you!" he shouts as my body explodes and milks his cock.

He peers down into my lust-hazy eyes. I lick my lips and taste him on my tongue. His essence. His vitality. Blood is equally favorable, and honestly more preferred, than his cum. His blood in me…

We are one.

One unit bonded together by love and lust and desires and actions and addictions and blood. He will always be mine. I will always be his.

And although I don't need to, when he withdraws, I drag my fingers up my slit and paint my palm with his cum. I bring it to my lips and rub where his blood was moments ago. Hooded eyes stare down at me. Two dark pools of pure, carnal need. Then, I part my lips and suck my fingers and taste both of us.

My eyes roll back in my head when he growls. "Do you need me to fuck you again, babe? Because if you keep that shit up, we'll be fucking all night."

I stare up at him with doe eyes. "Fuck me. But on my hands and knees, so I can look at them."

His eyes darken as his dick hardens against my thigh. "Yes, ma'am."

Quickly, he flips me on my belly, turns me so I face the seven bodies on the floor, hikes my ass in the air and fucks me senseless. And in this moment, I don't recall ever being more turned on before. At this rate, we will be fucking all night.

CHAPTER EIGHTEEN

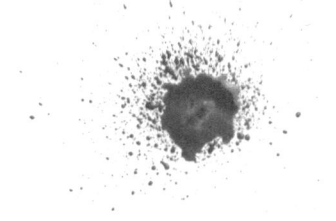

A SCREAM FILLED the air as she orgasmed for the fourth time in the last hour. His hands fisted her hips aggressively. Blood spilled out of small incisions where his nails bit her skin. She reached around and pressed down on his hands, indicating to fuck her harder.

He pumped in and out of her with hostility and greed. Greed for her. Greed for her pussy. Greed for the blood they spilled together. She forced herself back, meeting him thrust for thrust until he let go inside of her again. Her hand dove between her legs and grabbed his balls. She rolled and yanked them as he reached the tail end of his release.

When she let go, they collapsed on the mattress and laughed, still connected at the groin. They stared at each other for a long, drawn-out moment before either spoke.

"D, fuck babe. Think you broke my brain. Don't know what to fucking say."

She gazed into his eyes, brought a hand to his jaw and skimmed the rough, dark stubble. "You don't need to say a word, J. I know what goes through that magnificent brain of yours." She tapped her index finger on his temple.

"This has been the most intense one yet. How long until the next?" Urgency laced his words. His lust for carnage was a mad, hungry beast.

"Soon. I promise. Already have candidates lined up and have been watching them a few weeks. The next round won't have as many, but I'm adding another guy in the mix."

He locked eyes with her as his irises went black. He wrapped a hand around his flaccid dick and jerked to wake it up for another round.

"You know I love it when you bring guys in the mix. Knowing you can overpower them makes me hard as fuck." He stroked his growing erection. "Knowing you like to watch people fuck also gets me hard. Knowing we both get off on them not making it out of here alive… no fucking words, babe."

She stared at him as he stroked himself a moment. Her fingers dipped down to her entrance. Stroke for stroke, they kept pace with each other. A few strokes from climax, they were stirred from their hypnotic state when the doorbell rang.

They looked at one another, puzzled. She got up from the bed and stepped over to the computer, flicking through the camera screens until the front door came into view.

Two police officers stood at the door. Both men had their holsters unlatched and hands ready to draw their weapon. One of the officers reached out and knocked on the door, followed by a loud announcement.

"Police department. Open the door, please."

A wicked grin spread across her face. This hadn't been

her first run-in with the police. She was still here—confident—and didn't let the cops deter her. She informed J who their visitors were, momentarily distracted as he sat on the edge of the bed and stroked himself.

"Going to go deal with them. You staying in here?"

He nodded, then tipped his head back and groaned. He tugged his dick harder. D shook her head, but watched his hand with lascivious eyes.

"You better not get off while I deal with them." Her words a ten-inch blade—sharp and unyielding.

"No worries, babe. Just priming myself for you." He points to the monitor. "I'll watch you in action from here. By the time you get back, I'll be ready for another round."

She nodded then clicked on the computer a few times before exiting the room. She walked through the house, every room looking pristine and untouched. Steps before she reached the door, she heard the officer pounding his fist against the grain again and belting out the same words as before.

"Almost there."

Unlocking the deadbolt, she twisted the knob and opened the door. Both of the male officers stepped back, mouths agape. She took a step in their direction, propped a hand on the doorjamb, and asked, "How can I help you, gentlemen?"

It took both of the officers a moment to collect their thoughts. Their faces shell-shocked by the visual display. One of them spoke up with a stutter on his lips. "M-Ma'am… could y- you please put some clothes on."

She plastered on a confused expression then peered

down her body. Her eyes met theirs with a sparkle of sin glinting at the edges.

"No, I feel better without clothing. Plus, you interrupted me and were pretty insistent I answer. So here I am."

One of the officers swallowed with difficulty and averted his eyes. "Ma'am, we received calls from a couple of people tonight. Calls regarding a cry for help coming from your home."

She widened her devilish grin. "That was me. My husband and I like to role-play during sex. I was playing the helpless and defenseless damsel in distress. Can get him for you, but he isn't wearing clothes either."

Both officers put their hands up to stop her. "No ma'am. That won't be necessary." Both men took a small step back on the porch.

"Or, if you gentlemen would like, you can come in." She dragged her lower lip between her teeth. "I can always use more strong bodies against mine."

And with that, the officers took a few more steps in retreat. "That won't be necessary, ma'am. We just needed to follow up on the call and make sure no one was in distress. We will leave you and your husband to whatever it is you were doing. Have a great evening."

As the two officers walked down the steps and stepped on to the path, she called out. "Are you certain I can't convince you to stay?"

Both men turned to face her and gaped. D had her legs spread and fingers circling her clit. They stopped dead in their tracks, glanced at each other then back to her. Their professionalism slowly tipped and fell off the fence. The urge to stand their ground was strong, but their primal nature was much stronger.

Officer one glanced at officer two and spoke low enough for only him to hear. "Fuck, man. Do you think anyone will check on us for the next ten or fifteen minutes? Because my dick is hard as stone right now."

They studied one another for a beat. Exchanged a silent agreement before locking eyes with the woman on the porch. She slipped her fingers inside herself, fisted the doorjamb, and audibly panted. Officer two spoke up. "Think we'll be good for at least fifteen. Maybe more."

The two men headed back toward the house, straightened their spines, and walked with confidence and hunger. Inches away, officer one asked, "How can we assist you, ma'am?"

One hand still worked between her thighs as she brought the other to her breast and pinched and twisted the nipple. Breath heavy, she whispered, "I'd love for you to *come* inside."

She walked backward as the two followed in her wake. She took officer one's hand and placed it on her breast. Then took officer two's hand and put it between her legs. The two men fondled and licked and primed her body. Fingers pinched nipples. While others dipped in and out of her folds.

She fisted each of their cocks through their uniforms and squeezed urgently. "I want you to fuck me. Both of you. At the same time."

They glanced at each other as every man's fantasy flickered in their eyes.

She guided them to the couch and peeled away their uniforms. Within minutes, both men were naked in front of her. She forced one to sit on the couch before dropping to her knees and wetting his dick. Once satisfied, she made him lie back while she sucked the second man.

After both men were coated with her saliva, she climbed over the man on the couch and straddled his cock. Her folds spread wide as she slid down on his shaft. She rode his cock for a moment—adjusting to someone new—before peeking over her shoulder and asking the other if he was ready. He acquiesced and she bent over, exposing her ass to him. She spit into her hand and smeared it over the tight pucker between her cheeks. For a moment, she teased the tender spot to show him she wanted it.

He leaned forward, lined himself up, and penetrated the place most deem as forbidden. After a few dips in and out, his cock plunged deep in her ass. Both men gave pause before setting a rhythm which allowed one of them inside as the other slipped out. Moans and cries floated through the air. D pinched one nipple while the man beneath her sucked the other.

She stared at the man under her then back to the man behind her before seeing *her* man out of the corner of her eye.

She groaned as speech scraped her throat. "Hope you boys can keep up. I'm a challenging woman to please."

The two men exchanged a look of momentary confusion before challenge and determination took over. Just as they both pistoned their hips harsher, J walked up to the couch and slapped his cock in her face. His hand stroked with fevered energy. She opened her mouth and drooled for his dick.

One man fucked her face, one fucked her cunt, and one fucked her ass. Her body ignited and exploded. J twisted her nipples tightly between his fingers. As her orgasm settled, she dropped her mouth away a moment.

"You better fuck me harder. I expect at least two more orgasms before you get yours."

With the challenge laid out, the three men got to work. Stimulating every orifice and pleasure point of her body. Fingers rubbed her clit. Nails scraped down her spine. Tits and nipples manipulated in every way possible. Her orgasm detonated again. The men held out as long as they could while pounding viciously into her.

"Switch," she whispered.

Within seconds, her man laid below her and the officer was on her tongue. Different sensations. Different rhythms. She tasted her orgasm on him and it ignited her next immediately. As the third hit, the men chased their own release.

Before she granted it to each of them, she warned, "I expect your cum inside me. No pulling out."

With this, they each growled or groaned. And a vicious pounding commenced. An all-out fuck fest. As if it were a race to see who finished first. The first explosion hit her tongue. The second spurted in her ass. And the finale from J.

Moments passed. Breathing settled. Quietness filled the room.

She looked up from J and turned to face both of the officers with a wicked gleam in her eyes.

"See gentlemen, there is nothing to worry about here. Just a girl trying to get her brains fucked out. Which has been a pleasure. Stop by anytime. I would love to do this again in the future."

Hint taken, the two officers dressed back in their uniforms and headed for the door. Once they reached the car, they both took a minute to absorb what just happened. Officer one sat in the driver's seat and broke the silence first.

"Holy shit, man! That was fucking insane."

"No words, man. But I'm telling you right now... the next time this house comes up as some sort of disturbance call, we're calling first dibs before anyone else."

"Fucking right we are."

The car started and, a moment later, the two officers drove away, none the wiser. Oblivious to the seven bodies. Oblivious to the fact those seven bodies lay dead only thirty feet from where they were. Oblivious to the fact they just fucked their killer.

They drove away with permanent smiles on their faces while D and J continued their fuckfest and planned the next group's demise. It felt like the end, but it was only the beginning.

THANK YOU

Thank you so much for reading *By Dawn*. If you wouldn't mind taking a moment to leave a review on the retailer site where you made your purchase and/or Goodreads, it would mean the world to me.

Much love,
    Persephone

BY DAWN PLAYLIST

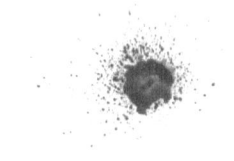

Here are some of the songs from the *By Dawn* playlist. You can listen to the entire playlist on Spotify!

The Final Seduction ∣ Alan Silvestri
First to Fall ∣ Brandon Boone
Lacrimosa ∣ Jason Graves
The Empty Doll ∣ Lucas King
Hall of Mirrors ∣ Benjamin Wallfisch

MORE BY PERSEPHONE

Typically, Persephone writes romance (contemporary and suspense).

Depths Awakened

A small town romance which captivates you from the start. Mags and Geoff are two broken souls who have sworn off love. Vowed to never lose anyone else. But their undeniable attraction brings them together and refuses to let go.

Distorted Devotion

Free-spirited Sarah lives life to the fullest. When a new love interest enters her life, she starts receiving strange gifts and letters. She doesn't want to relinquish her freedom or new love, but fears the consequences.

Undying Devotion

A long-term couple, Christy and Rick, live in a world of

secrets. Their friends envy the bond they share, but remain oblivious to their lifestyle and how deep the bond lies. Until a turn of events has Christy wanting to open up.

Beloved Devotion

Liz asks the love of her life, Tiffany, to marry her. When Tiffany hesitates, but says yes, Liz is determined to learn why. As the pieces start to fall in place, Liz discovers she doesn't know her fiancée at all.

Ink Veins

A collection of poetry written over the span of a decade.

ABOUT THE AUTHOR

 Author Persephone Autumn lives in Florida with her wife, crazy dog, and two lover-boy cats. A proud mom with a cuckoo grandpup. An ethnic food lover who has fun discovering ways to veganize her favorite non-vegan foods. If given the option, she would intentionally get lost in nature.

For several years, Persephone always did some form of writing—mostly journaling or poetry. After pairing her poetry with images and posting them online, she began the journey of writing her first novel.

Writer of mostly romance novels, on occasion she likes to dip her toes in other works. Future publications include poetry, and a psychological horror under P. Autumn.

CONNECT WITH PERSEPHONE

Connect with Persephone

www.persephoneautumn.com

Subscribe to Persephone's newsletter

www.persephoneautumn.com/newsletter

Join Persephone's Reader Group

Persephone's Playground

Follow Persephone Online

instagram.com/persephoneautumn

facebook.com/persephoneautumnwrites

goodreads.com/persephoneautumn

bookbub.com/authors/persephone-autumn

amazon.com/author/pautumn

pinterest.com/persephoneautumn

twitter.com/PersephoneAutum

ACKNOWLEDGMENTS

Thank you to the group chat who inspired this book. Nellie, Kristine, Scott, Jill, Brenda, and Jessica—your annoying behavior made it possible for me to find a way to kill you all and not go to jail. I hope you all loved your death—I know I did.

Let's not forget Nanci, who all but begged to die in this book. You're welcome. Glad I could be of service.

Thank you Ellie and Rosa at My Brother's Editor. Both of you are magical. This book started as a hot mess. And even after I cleaned it up, it was still a mess… until you made it pretty. All the hugs.

Thank you to my advanced readers and promo team. This book is far from what I usually publish, but it makes my heart happy that you read my words and helped me promote By Dawn.

Thank you Abigail Davies, for designing the cover and putting a face to By Dawn.

Thank you to every reader who picks up this book and reads it. By Dawn is far from conventional horror, but there are no rules when it comes to the story in your head.